Jazz Ford

The Alpha's Mate And The Vampire King

Book Three of The Alpha Series.

Jazz Ford

Jazz Ford

ISBN: 978-0-6452231-6-3

DEDICATION

I dedicate this book to anyone who needs a little magic in their lives.

Jazz Ford

Chapter 1

Nina kisses my cheek and takes a seat at the desk beside me.

'Magnus, is there anything else I can do for you?'

'Could you please hand me the Shady Crest status report?' I say as I set aside a pile of paperwork that I had just finished signing on the desk.

Rolling up her sleeve, Nina waves her wand 'Lifto Levitatous', she says. The paper rises and swirls in a circular pattern, one page at a time, before settling in a neat stack in front of me.

'Nina, it was literally in front of you. You could have just reached for it, you know?'

'Well, where's the fun in that?' she gives a warm smile.

'Do you suppose you could conjure me up a mug of coffee, by any chance?' I grin.

'Magnus, you realise I'm not capable of doing that?'

'Honestly, I'm not sure what you are capable of yet. You read that spellbook each night and refuse to tell me what you've learnt.'

'Well, you have to admit that seeing me cast the spell rather than listening to me explain it is far more interesting.'

'That's true, but it is a shame there is no conjuring a coffee spell in that book.' I chuckle.

We hear a disturbance coming from downstairs.

'Where is he? Where is Alpha Magnus?' A man demands.

Hank storms into the office and slams his fist on my desk before Nina, and I can even get up.

He cries, 'You, you liar, you cheat!'

I smile as I cross my arms and relax back in my chair.

'Hank, it's great to hear from you. How may I assist you?'

He steels himself at my words.

'How can you assist? I'll explain how you can assist! My sister Addison was supposed to be your Mate and the Luna of Shadow Crest. Instead, you betrayed our agreement and sought your soul mate.'

'Are you referring to the contract you blackmailed me into? Where you threatened to reveal Nina's secret to everyone, knowing it would put her in grave danger?'

Nina rises to her feet, her hands on her hips.

'Hank, are you aware of how ridiculous you sound right now? She growls, 'You're lucky we didn't toss you into werewolf jail for blackmailing an Alpha! You are exiled from Shadow Crest. Now get out and don't return.'

'Or what?' Hank squints.

Nina casts her spell with a flourish of her wand. She exclaims, 'Repeliate!' Hank is pushed back against the wall with an unseen force. Nina approaches him as he rises from his seat on the floor. 'Or I'll transform you into a frog,' she cautions.

Hank shakes and bolts out the door.

I walk over to Nina, 'Repeliate, hey?' I say to Nina. I give her a high-five and remark, 'I like that one.'

'Me too,'

'It must be lunchtime for sure?' my tummy grumbles with hunger.

Nina smiles as she says, 'Yep, the last one downstairs is a rotten egg.'

'Game on.' I say, and then I hear Nina behind me as I rush out the door. 'Skedaddle Dash,' she says. When I turn around, she's gone.

My mouth hangs wide in surprise that she cheated using a spell. I make my way downstairs to see Nina sitting in her seat with the biggest grin.

Nina chuckles, 'Oh, look, it's the rotten egg.'

Zak, Pipsqueak, Gianna, Flint, May and Josie try to keep their giggles to themselves.

'Nina, you can't use your magic and blink to win the race,'

She shrugs, picks up her fork, and eats her lunch.

'We should have a bonfire tonight?' Flint proposes.

'That sounds like it would be a lot of fun,' Nina says.

'I'll bring the marshmallows,' Josie squeals.

'Well, that settles it, a bonfire it is.' I say.

I take Nina's hand after we complete our lunch. 'Let's go for a run with our wolves,'

'Great!' My wolf has been pleading with me to let her out all morning.'

We leave the packhouse and remove our clothes outside the woods. Nina shifts into her black wolf while I shift into my white wolf. When I get close enough, I lick the white star symbol on her forehead. The race begins when she nuzzles me back.

As the wind whips through our fur, we leap over logs and fallen branches. We sprint in and out of the trees, trying to outrun each other. We don't stop running for hours until arriving at our favourite area, Shadow Lake. We both dive in and swim back to the surface in human form. My heart is bursting with happiness as I gaze into her eyes. I'm so lucky she is my Mate. I could never be happier than I am right now.

Before drying off and returning to the packhouse for the bonfire, I give her a soft kiss.

While Flint rolls a few logs closer for everyone to sit on, Zak has gathered logs and branches in a half metal barrel.

'I'll go inside and get the marshmallows.' Josie says.

May appears with Josie, and the two of them sit together.

'Well, I guess I'd better get this fire going.' Flint says.

'Inferno Flamo!' exclaims May, igniting the fire.

'Or I suppose May will get it started, I guess…,' Flint replies nervously.

Nina is cuddled on my lap, staring at the fire with me. I wrap a blanket around her. Her head lies on my chest.

The fire crackles and embers hover above it.

Nina murmurs, 'Inferno Flamo.' The flames coalesce and develop into a dynamic image of a galloping horse.

'Wow,' we all exclaim.

May says, 'Inferno Flamo,' embers mix to form the image of a dolphin leaping out of the flaming ocean.

'How does using these spells work? 'How do you have such control over the flames and embers?' I enquire.

'Well, we say Inferno Flamo for fire spells, then we picture what we want it to do, and it does it.' The Aqua Bedew spell and any other spell related to an element work the same way,' Nina explains.

'Ah, I see. What you and May are capable of is truly incredible,'

'It certainly is.' She smiles.

Suddenly thousands of more embers appear, creating a spectacular light show.

'That's amazing, Nina!' Josie expresses herself.

Nina responds, 'That's not me doing that.'

'I thought that was Nina?' Josie asks May.
'It wasn't me,' May says.
'If it wasn't either of you, then who is it?'
Steps approach from behind us. We all spring to our feet and prepare to shift.

Five people in olive green hooded cloaks come to a standstill. The individual in the centre takes a step in front of the others. I can't help but notice a Smokey coloured cat sitting beside one of the hooded people at the back.

Chapter 2

'Who are you? How did you get into my territory without us noticing?'

The person in front lowers their hood.

'Yiselda?' I say.

'Alpha Magnus,' she murmurs before turning her focus on Nina. She acknowledges Nina with a smile and a nod. The four hooded people behind her all bow their heads to Nina.

Nina and I exchange a troubled look.

'What brings you here, Yiselda?' Nina inquires.

A mouse sits upon Yiselda's shoulder and begins to clean its whiskers.

'After all, Magnus, it's fantastic to see you were able to break the spell,' she replies, dismissing Nina's query.

'I did,' I admit. 'But I can't help but think that's not why you're here.'

'Alpha Magnus, I would like you to meet the Midnight Coven's members.

Introduce yourself to Fern, Ela Ria, and Lilac.' As their names are called out, the women drop their hoods.

They are all stunning women. Fern has brown hair and blue eyes. Ela has brown eyes and blonde hair. Ria has red hair, green eyes and numerous freckles. There is a cream-coloured snake around her neck. I try not to squirm thinking about the snake. Then there is Lilac, her hair is black, and her eyes are brown.

'It's a pleasure to meet you all. Please have a seat,' I say, motioning to the wooden logs.

They warm themselves by the fire and make themselves comfortable.

'So, The Midnight Coven?' I question.

'That's correct. We are the last known coven, although only a few people are aware of us. We learned about Nina and her sister. They are half-wolf, half-witch hybrid.' Yiselda looks at Nina.

'I knew there was something special about you when I saw you, but I couldn't put my finger on what it was, but I can see it now, all around you. The curse must have been shadowing your power from everyone. The rumour that Nina and her sister are witches spread quickly. There's a reason we're the only witches remaining and why we've remained hidden from the rest of the world.'

'Can you tell me why?' I enquire.

Yiselda inhales deeply. 'Witch hunts,' She whispers, sending eerie shivers down my spine.

'But now the eggs are out of the basket, werewolves are aware that witches still exist, and Nina is your mate, making things quite interesting. So, my midnight coven sisters have become hopeful that they may be able to come out of hiding and live peacefully among the pack, your pack.'

Zak and Josie take a step back in surprise, tripping over the log. We all exchange glances as we hear nothing but a croak, followed by another croak and another. As the croaking comes from Ela, we all look at her oddly. She giggles and reaches into her pocket for a slimy toad.

'Everyone, it's fine.' That noise isn't coming from me. It's simply Todd, my familiar. He's a toad,' Ela exclaims as though it's the greatest thing ever.

I try not to cringe and instead frown.

'So, you all want to live here in Shadow Crest?' I ask.

They all nod and smile except for Yiselda.

'I'm afraid I wouldn't be able to stay. The four girls would be the only ones residing here. Perhaps if the other packs see that we can coexist peacefully in this pack with you, they will rethink their ideas about witches and allow us to live freely without fear?'

'This is a significant decision that Nina and I can't make right now. Tomorrow, we'll have a meeting and seek counsel from our elders.'

'We would appreciate that, Alpha Magnus.'

'Why wouldn't you be able to stay, Yiselda?'

'The Covenstead we live in is more than just a house. We have creatures and beings that have been sealed inside and can never be released. One of us must remain at the Covenstead to ensure that the ward spells are not removed.'

'What kind of beings are they?' I ask.

'Creatures you hope you'll never meet, the darkest beings you can envision. Grimghouls and Shadow Reapers, that come from your deepest darkest nightmares. It would be like opening Pandora's box if they were set free. Because of this, it became the name of our Covenstead.'

'Your home is known as Pandora's Box?' I grimace.

Fern, Ela, Ria, and Lilac chuckle and nod, amused at the situation.

'Yes, if only your species could understand that witches are here to protect everyone, to keep the world free of demons and dark forces. We must keep anyone who wants to bring us harm locked up by having wards and spells in place. We also create potions to help heal the sick.'

'Won't you be lonely staying in Pandora's box?' Nina asks.

Yiselda laughs, 'I wish. But unfortunately, the Vampire King never shuts up. I've already put up with him for a few centuries as it is. Fern, Ela, Ria and Lilac can come by anytime if they are able to reside here. They could teleport to Pandora's Box easily enough each day if they wanted to.'

'Vampire King?' I mind-link to Nina.

'Never knew vampires existed, let alone a king?' She mind-links back.

Chapter 3

'However, enough with Pandora's Box. We want to invite Nina and May to join our coven as sisters. Joining us also means that it will be our responsibility to protect and keep each other safe in times of peril,'

'But Nina and May are part of the Shadow Crest pack,'

'Because they are half-witch, half-wolf, they can be part of both. This would also unify us as one prominent coven or, as you call it, pack.'

'I appreciate it, Yiselda.' At tomorrow's meeting, May and I will discuss it. Let's get to know each other a little better in the meanwhile and roast some marshmallows?' Nina proposes.

We're all holding our sticks, placed above the fire with marshmallows. Then Yiselda works her magic and puts on a performance for us to enjoy.

We watch a little bird who is still unable to fly like her siblings. However, the little bird does not give up and continues to attempt to fly every day. She eventually learns to fly and flies past her siblings.

We applaud Yiselda for the charming story.

'Thank you for your kindness, but we must depart. We'll be back here at midnight tomorrow,' Yiselda adds. She then draws a circle on the ground with a star within and sets five stones at each point of the star.

Fern, Ela, Ria, and Lilac vanish as they enter the circle. Yiselda sends out one more wave before stepping in and disappearing.

'That was just as entertaining to see as the show she just created,' According to Flint.

‘How do you feel about joining as one pack?’ I ask Nina.

'It wouldn't feel right to dismiss them. It must be disheartening to have been in hiding for so long. Magnus, I sympathise with them.'

'It's the same for me. Ultimately, as Alpha and Luna, the decision is ours, but I believe some assistance and advice from our parents wouldn't hurt?'

'I agree,' she adds, gently kissing my cheek.

The next day we arranged a pack meeting.

Leon and Amelia are the first to arrive. Ever since Nina and I became the Luna and Alpha of the pack, all our parents relocated. They still live in Shadow Crest but are now all in their own homes closer to the woods.

With our parents sitting at the table and Nina by my right side, and my Beta Zak by my left, I begin the meeting.

'I appreciate everyone's attendance at this meeting. You're probably all wondering why you're here. We received an unexpected proposal last night. I'm sure you all remember Yiselda?'

Everyone nods.

'Yes, she helped rid you of your fever.' Mother says.

'She came to see us last night, bringing four other witches with her. They desire to unite with the werewolf society and join our pack now that word of Nina and May being half-witch has spread.'

Ryker and Leon exchange worried looks.

'Did you say anything to them?' My father inquires.

'I told them I'd call a meeting and talk about it, and here we are,'

'Personally, son, I don't have a problem with it. We love them, Nina and May, regardless that they are hybrids. My only concern is how the other packs will take this information and how they will handle it. It won't surprise me if most packs are against the idea,'

'We haven't considered the ramifications from other packs. Yiselda hopes if they can see us living in peace, they will perhaps adjust to the idea and realise witches aren't as dangerous as they have always believed,'

'I'm fine with it too, but I'm concerned that it might backfire and endanger Nina and May's safety,' Leon explains.

'They may not like that Nina and May being half-witch, remain in our pack. But it will be a safety issue for them anyway,' I say.

'You're right, son. That is something we will have to be wary about,'

'If they join us, Nina and May will also join their coven, which means the midnight coven will protect them. If the wolves come for Nina and May, we'll need the witches' help to protect them. We can fight most packs, but we wouldn't stand a chance if they all fought simultaneously,' I say.

Everyone agrees with a nod.

'It has been determined that the Midnight Coven will join us.' I announce.

Before departing, everyone rises and bows to Nina and me.

Chapter 4

Nina and I walk into town to meet up with Shadow Crest's local pack members. Although the majority of the group has accepted Nina's half-witch status, a few members remain concerned about her abilities.

Mrs Turnpot is squatting in her vegetable garden as we come to a halt at a small picket gate.

Nina pokes Mrs Turnpot over the fence and says, 'Hello, Mrs Turnpot.'

When Mrs Turnpot notices Nina, she glances up at us and falls back.

'Oh!' she trembles and retreats.

'Mrs Turnpot, what are you planting today?' Nina is overjoyed.

'C-Carrots,' she replies, 'but they haven't been growing.'

Nina takes a look around the garden. 'Perhaps I can assist? Revito Sprouto,' she says.

Mrs Turnpot's carrots are sprouting and growing right before our eyes.

'Thank you, Luna, thank you. Mrs Turnpot says as she vigorously shakes Nina's hand.

'No problem, Mrs Turnpot, I'll see you later,' Nina smiles.

We resume walking.

'How long have you known that spell?' I enquire.

'A few nights ago. You're the first to see me cast it.' She smiles. 'I'm excited the Midnight Coven will be joining our pack. Imagine all the spells I'll learn? I can't wait to see how they make their potions too! And those little pets, they seem to all have one? I must ask them tonight if having a pet is part of being a witch?'

'I'm concerned about that snake. I'm shocked the toad and mouse haven't been eaten. I'm curious whether it's been tempted too, though.' I say.

'Are you really going to ask them that, Magnus?'

'What? I'm curious,'

'Yeah, and you know how curiosity killed the cat?' We both burst out laughing.

'Hey, since we are near the library, I have a surprise,'

'A surprise for me?' Nina exclaims.

'Come on,' I say, taking her hand in mine. I escort her into the library.

As we stroll past everyone, we say, 'Hello, good day.'

I approach the librarian.

'Miss Smith, it's great to see you again. I'd like to borrow the library keys,' She gives me an odd look and takes her keys off her belt.

She hands over the keys and adds, 'Sure, Alpha Magnus,'

'Thank you,' I say as I recapture Nina's hand, head to the forbidden door, and unlock it.'

'Alpha, Magnus, Alpha! You are not permitted to enter.' Miss Smith expresses her anxiety by saying, 'No one is allowed in the restricted area,'

'I'm the Alpha, Miss Smith. I'm free to do whatever I want, and I'm in charge and responsible for this place,' I explain.

She gives me a timid nod and moves back, not daring to look into the forbidden room.

I shut the door behind us, and it's as gloomy as it was the last time.

'Do you think you could do the honours and provide us with some light so we can see?' I ask Nina.

She takes her wand from her pocket and flicks the tip, causing a small flame to appear. Unfortunately, seeing the entire room is not possible.

'Illumini!' she exclaims. The flame grows larger, filling the room with light. 'Wow! This is incredible. I had no idea this room existed.' She runs her fingers across the spines of the books and exclaims, 'These books must be thousands of years old.' Then, she sets her wand in an empty candle holder on the vast stone table in the centre of the room.

'Surprise,' I say, folding my arms and leaning against the stone wall as she surveys the room. 'I was hoping you'd want to take a look at the books and bring one home to study? Unfortunately, no one has been allowed to access or read these texts because magic has always been prohibited,' I add, endearingly looking at Nina.

'Magnus, thank you so much,' she says as she rushes over to me and softly kisses my lips.

'You're welcome,' I say, beaming.

Nina selects ten books and carries them to the stone table, where she begins scanning them. Finally, she sets aside the sixth book, returns the others, and delivers me the one she desires.

I read the title aloud: 'A book of potions.' I smirk and say, 'Why am I not surprised?'

Nina laughs and shrugs her shoulders, amused. I return the book to her and then raise the keys. As I remove the key to this room, she keeps an eye on me. There's a slender chain amongst the other miscellaneous stuff on the disorganised stone table. I step behind Nina and hook the chain through the loop at the top of the key. As I carefully wrap it around her neck, she gasps.

'This room is now yours, and you can use it whenever you want,'

'Magnus, I'm at a loss for words,'

'How about you say I love you?' I offer with a chuckle.

'Magnus, I love you,' she says as she holds my face in both hands and kisses my lips. She gives a kind smile.

She says, 'Dimulous,' while holding her book in one hand and recovering her wand with the other. Her wand goes out, and the room becomes dark once more. We walk out the door, and she reaches down to lock it with the key dangling from her neck.

'Magnus, this is incredible. We're forming an alliance with witches. I'm going to join a coven, and I've got my own secret room with all the magic literature I could want,' she exclaims.

'I would do anything for you, Nina. I would give you the whole world if I could. I'd even give you the moon,' I say, gazing into her beautiful doe eyes.

'Oh, Magnus. To me, you are everything. You are the whole world and the whole moon,' she whispers.

We kiss passionately, only for bystanders in the library to begin clapping and wolf-whistling at us.

'Shh, this is a library. Everyone needs to be silent,' Miss Smith scowls at everyone.

Before we leave the library, I return the ring of keys to Miss Smith, minus the key to the forbidden room.

Chapter 5

We see Zak and Pipsqueak stapling fliers to lampposts across town, telling Shadow Crest of our upcoming merger with the Midnight Coven pack.

The pack huddles together to read the posts. They are unsure what to make of it. Nina and I approach them in the hopes of reassuring them.

'Hello everyone,' Nina says, smiling. They all smile politely.

'I want to reassure everyone that joining forces with the Midnight coven is a beneficial move. Extra aid around town would be beneficial, as would magical protection if our community were ever in danger. Witches are not to be feared. Your loving Luna is one, along with her sister May and has never caused us any harm. They are on our side and want to live peacefully amongst us and help keep humans and us safe from any threats to our communities. You are all welcome to join us at midnight tonight if you wish to.'

Everyone nods and smiles at each other, and all appear to be more at ease.

***

It's nearly midnight. Everyone in the packhouse is staring at the circle with the stones at each point of the star.

'How does this work? Do you believe they will materialise in the circle, or will a cloud of mist emanate from within and cause them to appear?' May asks.

'I suppose we'll find out any minute now,' Nina adds.

Yiselda is the first to emerge in a flash, followed by Fern, Ela, Ria, and Lilac, right on the stroke of midnight.

Yiselda grins as she notices half of the village staring in wonder.

'I assume you consented to join us as one community?' Yiselda inquires.

'Welcome back,' I say, 'Yes, we are all thrilled to have you join us. Nina and May are also delighted to join your coven and become your sisters.' My parents stand amongst the crowd and smile at me.

'Let's begin the initiation then and have you join our pack.

An athame with a black wood handle is brought forward. I take the knife and cut across the palm of Yiselda's hand and then across my palm. We clasp our hands together.

'I, Alpha Magnus, of the Shadow Crest Pack, with the Moon Goddess as our witness, accept the midnight coven into our pack. Wolf and Witch have merged.'

Lightning hits, and thunder roars with the same ferocity as it did the night I accidentally cursed Nina.

'The Moon Goddess has blessed us,' I declare aloud.

We part hands to find our wounds have all but healed.

Everyone cheers and shouts their welcome to the witches of the midnight coven.

The little mouse crawls out from Yiselda's hood and sits on her shoulder.

'I have to ask you, Yiselda, these pets you all have. Is it part of being a witch to have one?' Nina asks.

Yiselda laughs, 'These are not just pets, my dear. These are our familiars. This mouse is not just a mouse. Nibbler gives me a source of extra power when I need it. I can see through her eyes and hear through her ears at any time. She also helps me with potions and ingredient gathering. She is a unique familiar since she can transform into many animals. Her choice appears to be a mouse in general. I'm guessing it's due to her fondness for cheese,' Yiselda chuckles.

'How would May and I receive a familiar?'

'Well, at your and May's initiation into our coven, a portal to Silverfay forest will open. All of the familiars' dwell there. You'll trek through the woods until you come across your familiar. You'll know when you've discovered yours, much like a mate bond. You will feel a deep connection and be pulled to each other. When you touch your familiar, your wand and clothes will alter, and the mark of your familiar will appear on your chest.'

'Like a bite mark?' Nina says with a cringe.

'Not at all. It will be a symbol like a tattoo,' Yiselda explains.

'Oh, I was worried for a moment there,' Nina says with relief.

'So was I,' I add, not liking the notion of anyone else marking my Mate with a bite.

'This is so exciting,' May exclaims. 'I wonder what familiar I'll get?'

'If you want to find out, we can start the ceremony?' Yiselda smiles.

'Yes, let's start the ceremony. I'm ready,' Nina says.

The five witches stand in a circle, 'Nina, May, come forth and join us,' Yiselda says. Nina and May approach the circle of witches. They all hold hands.

'Once the portal opens, that is when you can let go of our hands and enter Silverfay Forest.' Yiselda instructs.

The rest of the pack and I take a few steps back to give them more space.

Yiselda begins the ceremony.

'Thy coven sprouts like a seed.

Mother Earth, we beseech thee to acknowledge our two new sisters, like branches budding and flowers blossoming

add them to our tree.

Thy new sisters of Midnight Coven, we welcome thee.'

We listen to Yiselda say the words to initiate May and Nina into the coven. The earth trembles as a swirl of dazzling mist encircles them, and grass and flowers bloom about their feet.

The mist dissolves, and a spark of light appears inside the circle, becoming increasingly visible with each passing second. It is the entrance to Silverfay forest.

Yiselda, Fern, Ela, Ria and Lilac all smile at Nina and May and nod for them to enter Silverfay forest.

Nina and May break the circle by releasing everyone's hands. Nina is the first to make her way to the gateway. Smiling, she takes a deep breath and vanishes into Silverfay forest, the realm of familiars. May is so excited that she doesn't hesitate and rushes in after Nina.

Chapter 6

Nina

I'm standing in the most enchanting gorgeous woodland I've ever seen. The trees are not just various colours of green but also pinks, purples, and blues. They generate a glow that gives the trees the appearance of being composed of diamonds. A silver mist floats in the air, glistening in the breeze.

May slams into the back of me out of nowhere.
'Sorry,' she chuckles as I stare her down. 'Wow! This place is beautiful.' She says.

We begin exploring and come across a variety of animals. A sloth climbs a tree slowly as a bat hangs upside down on a branch. A possum pokes its head out of a tree hollow.
'Hello,' I say, waving at the animals. May gives me a strange look, then comes to a standstill and

casts a glance to the left. 'I need to go this way,' she says.

I followed her until she kneeled beside a vast bush. 'Hello, my familiar, I feel you're around here somewhere?'

'I'm not sensing anything,' I say.

'That's because we're not yet close to your familiar.'

The brush rustles, and a Fennec fox emerges.

'This is the cutest thing I've ever seen!' May squeals with delight. 'Come forth, little one,' May reassures the young fox, 'I'm not going to hurt you.'

The fox approaches May and sits down in front of her. She extends her hand to pat the fox. A brilliant light swirl around them both the instant they make contact. I keep watching as they levitate. May's clothing shifts from slacks and a loose top to a dark brown tailored dress with a corset back as she hovers slightly above the ground. The hem and sleeves of the dress are embellished with stunning gold embroidery. Her wand appears to float in front of her. She leans out to accept it, and the wand produces another ray of light. Unlike the elaborate features on the other witch's wands, ours resemble sticks. May's wand changes. At the bottom, a silver swirl appears, accompanied with jewels and embellishments.

The Fennec Fox leaps onto May's shoulder and places its paw on her chest. May flinches and turns to face the fox. 'I can hear what you're thinking,' she says. The fox removes its paw and leaves its imprint.

May grins as she stares at me. 'Did you see everything that just happened?'

'Yes, that was the most incredible sight I've ever seen! You look great in your dress, and your familiar is cute,' I say, giving it a scratch behind the ear.

'Sabre says she likes you,' May laughs.

'Well, I like her as well,' I smile.

A portal appears out of nowhere. Yiselda can be seen on the other side. She motions for May to come forward.

'I think the portal reopened for you to return home?' I say to May.

'Good luck Nina. I'll be waiting for you on the other side,' she says, hugging me.

She hurries back through the portal before I can say anything. It closes immediately behind her.

I approach many of the animals but have no connection with them. So, I decide to venture further into the woods. I eventually reach a section of the woodland distinct from the others. It's dark and foreboding. The trees look to be lifeless and devoid of colour. It has nothing enchanting about it, but it seems natural as if I'm destined to be here. I can see a dim blue light further past the trees.

'You can do it, Nina, one step at a time,' I tell myself as I begin trudging over the muddy dirt, pushing dead twigs from the brittle branches out of my face.

The further I travel into the lifeless woods, the more vibrant the blue light becomes. Then, finally, I arrive at the most amazing tree I've ever seen. It has two gigantic branches that curve like tusks, leaving a large empty circle between them where the great blue moon in the sky shines through. It's an incredible sight.

A sliver of black mist flashes through the tree. I attempted to see what it was, but it moved too quickly. It whizzed past like a flash once more, this time closer. Whatever it is, it is as dark as night and has wings.

'I've been waiting for you for thousands of years,' he says in a deep voice, I can hear in my thoughts.

'Are you my familiar?' I ask. I already know the answer because I can feel the connection between us like an unseen rope that pulls us closer together.

'Why bother asking when you already know?' he responds.

'Can you read my mind?'

'Yes,'

'... Are you going to reveal yourself? I'd like to meet you properly,' I ask.

'You're not like the other witches, which explains why you'll be my master. The question is, how do you differ from the other witches? I sense your strength is far greater and also different to theirs.'

'Perhaps I should introduce myself properly? I'm Nina, mate to Alpha Magnus and Luna of the Shadow Crest pack. I am a hybrid. Half-wolf, half-witch,' I explain.

I undress, shift into my wolf, and let out a massive howl.

'Incredible,' he exclaims. Suddenly, a swoosh of black smoke drops in front of me. I revert to my human shape and gaze at the majestic raven in front of me. He does not appear to be a normal raven, though, since he emits black mist from his entire body.

'You are the most incredible raven I have ever seen,'

'That's because I'm not just raven nor just a familiar. I am the rarest and the oldest of them all. I am the Shadow Raven,'

'What is your name?' I ask whilst admiring him.

'Reaper.' He says, followed by a caw and flaps his wings.

'Well, Reaper, it's a pleasure to meet you, and I look forwards to our future endeavours together,' I smile. I'm ecstatic that Reaper is my familiar.

'Likewise, let us unite as one,' he says.

I extend my hand. A dazzling light spreads around us as soon as my fingertips brush Reaper's feathers. I ascend slightly above the ground, my clothes changing from a basic plain dress to a maroon-coloured fitted gown with a corset back. The sleeves of my dress grow long. Like the other witches' gowns, the hem and sleeves are decorated with gorgeous gold embroidery.

My wand materialises in front of me. As I reach out to take it, the wand emits another beam of light—my wand alters. At the bottom, a gold swirl appears as the wand becomes embellished with jewels and carvings.

Reaper lands on my shoulder. The dark mist emitted by him whirls in the air and rests below my collarbone, leaving his imprint. Reaper is now my familiar, and I, now his master.

Chapter 7

I'm feeling more powerful than I've ever felt before. My veins are filled with a fresh wave of energy.

'This power,' I murmur, twisting my head to look over my shoulder at Reaper. 'Does this come from you?'

Reaper squawks before responding over our mind-link.

'Yes, now that we're bonded, I can give you as little or as much power as you need.'

'Do you mean that what I'm feeling now isn't the whole extent of your power?'

'You mean our power, and no, not at all. Let's just pray that you'll never have to utilise the full amount.'

'What would happen if we had to utilise it all at once?'

'I'd very likely die.'

I take a breather. 'Well, I'll make a mental note not to absorb it all,' I say.
'We'll see,' Reaper says.

The portal to Shadow Crest has opened.
'It's time for you to meet your new family, Reaper.' I flash a smirk.
'Yes, I can't wait,' he answers unenthused.
'Don't be that way, Reaper. You'll adore them, and there are more familiars among the five other witches with whom you might enjoy their company. May, one of the witches, is my sister.'
'Excellent, more vexing familiars.'
I can't help but chuckle. 'You poor creature, Reaper, you've been alone for thousands of years, and now you'll have to suffer being surrounded by tons of love and friends.'

I pass through the portal, Reaper still on my shoulder, and return to Shadow Crest.

'Nina!' Magnus says. He moves to embrace me but pauses as Reaper flaps his wings, surprising Magnus. 'Wait, is your familiar supposed to have smoke flowing out of its feathers like that?' he inquires. Yiselda gasps and moves closer to inspect Reaper.

'It can't be? Isn't that the mythical Shadow Raven? I thought it was a fairytale.' She's taken aback.
'His name is Reaper. It's usual for him to emit black mist.' I grin.

He caws and flaps his wings again. I can see he's showing off. I try not to laugh.
May dashes over, carrying Sabre on her shoulder. We exchange glances and embraces. Reaper is irritated and caws loudly in May's ear.
'Ugh, you don't have to be rude, bird. Your master is my sister,' May pouts.
'His name is Reaper. You'll have to forgive him this once. I found him in the dead woods, far from all the other familiars, where he has spent thousands of years being anti-social,' I explain.
'Oh, I see. Well, it's great to meet you, Reaper. My name is May, and this is my familiar Sabre, the Fennec fox,' Reaper acknowledges her with a low caw.

Magnus and Yiselda turn and face the crowd. Yiselda clears her throat.
'It is done. We are now united, the first wolf-witch community to exist and live peacefully together. My sisters and I look forward to helping

maintain this wonderful township of Shadow Crest with you.'

Everyone applauds and cheers. Reaper flies off to a nearby tree while I run up to Magnus and kiss him endearingly.

Ryker and Astrid approach us.

'We are so proud of you, son. Uniting with the witches will set such a wonderful example for the other pack communities,' Ryker says to Magnus.

'Congratulations on your initiation into the Midnight Coven, Nina, and for your new little companion, Reaper,' Astrid says to me.

'Thank you. I don't know how I'm supposed to sleep with all this adrenaline and new power?'

'Perhaps shifting and going for a run with Magnus might help burn some of that excess energy away?' Astrid smiles.

'Yes, great idea,' I say. Magnus and I hug them both goodnight, and everyone returns to their homes.

'It's time for me to return to Pandora's box. I'm sure we'll see each other in the days ahead.' Yiselda says, bidding Fern, Ela, Ria, and Lilac farewell.

Their eyes well up with tears. They can still see Yiselda anytime they want, but it won't be the same as living with her in Pandora's Box. Yiselda enters the circle with the star and stones within and vanishes.

'Let us show you your new bedrooms in the packhouse,' I smile as I turn to see my new sisters. They perk up and walk into the packhouse with Magnus and me. We proceed upstairs and show them all the extra rooms down the hall from where Magnus and I sleep.

'Pick any room you like. The rooms are all identically sized rooms with their own bathrooms. The only difference is that the room colours are different.'

No one is surprised when Lilac chooses the purple room. Fern picks the green, Ela chooses the yellow and Ria the red room. May waves them and us goodnight and retreats to her room.

'We should get some sleep too,' Magnus says.

'I won't be able to sleep. I will need to shift and run all this new energy and power out of my system,' I explain.

'Do you want me to come with you?'

'Only if you aren't too tired too?'

'I'll be fine. Let's go.' He smiles.

We strip our clothes off in our bedroom, shift into our wolves, and dash downstairs and out the door. After a few minutes of running through the forest, Reaper is flying roughly fifty metres high above me.

'Enjoying the view of Shadow Crest?' I mind-link Reaper.

'No, where are all the dead trees? Why is everything so bright, colourful and….'

'Alive?' I complete his sentence and laugh.

'Yeah, that,' he says.

'Welcome to Shadow Crest Reaper, the town of werewolves and now witches. A place where everything flourishes and never dies.'

'Lucky me,' he replies, his usual unenthusiastic tone.

'I'm curious, where do familiars sleep?'

'They may go wherever they want. I used to sleep in the dead moon tree in Silverfay forest, but we're on our second lap around Shadow Crest, and there isn't a single dead tree in this entire town,'

'Well, let's go back home now that I've burned off some energy,' I say.

I pounced over Magnus a few times before returning to the packhouse. We run upstairs and shift back to our human forms. I put my nightgown on while Magnus puts on his shorts.

There is a tapping sound coming from our window. Magnus casts a curious glance at me, and I shrug. He looks out the window to see what's going on. Reaper enters the room, walks by Magnus, and flies onto the rail at the foot of our bed. I crawl into bed. Magnus is reluctant but jumps in. I put my head on his chest as he draws me into his arms.

Ten minutes have passed. When I open my eyes, Magnus is still completely awake.

'Is everything all right?' I ask.

'You don't believe your pet will stare at me all night like that, do you? He is creeping me out.'

I look down at the foot of our bed, and Reaper is eerily staring Magnus down.

'Reaper, seriously?' I say.

He caws and turns around with his back facing us. 'That's better, now everyone sleep, and my mate's eyes better still be in their sockets in the morning, Reaper or else I'll make you the brightest, most colourful birdhouse full of rainbows and glitter and force you to sleep in it,' I warn.

'You truly are wicked, Master,' Reaper replies as he caws angrily and nuzzles his beak beneath his wing before falling asleep.

Chapter 8

It started around 7 a.m. with a series of caws. Magnus puts a pillow over his face and his ears. Unlike Magnus, I take my pillow and fling it at Reaper. As the pillow knocks him off the foot of our bed, his Caw switches to a squawk.

'Good morning to you too, Master,' he hisses via the mind-link.

'You're a Raven, not a Rooster, Reaper!' I growl.

Magnus chuckles but stops as Reaper shoots him a death glare. I grab Magnus' pillow and toss it at Reaper, missing him by a centimetre.

'And stop staring at Magnus in that manner,' I say.

'Fine, I'm hungry for grubs anyway,' he adds before flying out the window.

I roll onto Magnus, and we kiss and snuggle for a few moments before getting ready for the day. We can hear Fern, Ela, Ria, and Lilac giggling as they go down the stairs. When I opened my door,

Lilac slides down the railing backwards. 'Skedaddle Dash,' Ela exclaims and vanishes. Ria races down the stairs while Fern leaps over the balustrade and skips half the steps. Magnus and I make our way down the stairs and into the dining room.

'Lifto Levitatious,' says Ela. Magnus and I watch as the sugar dish drifts over towards her. She takes a teaspoon of sugar from the bowl and sprinkles it on top of her cereal. Then she flicks her wand, relocating the bowl to its original location on the table.

'Good morning,' I address everyone at the table.

'Good morning, Luna,' everyone greets me.

'I hope you all had a good night's sleep.' Magnus asks.

'Yes, Alpha Magnus, we did thank you,' Ria adds.

May yawns as she walks into the dining area and takes a seat. Sabre circles the dining room a few times before jumping up and resting on a window ledge.

'Do you have any plans for today?' I ask the witches.

'We were thinking about touring the town centre to meet more people,' Fern explains.

'That sounds fantastic,' I smile.

We wave goodbye as they 'Skedaddle Dash' into town.

'We have a lot of paperwork to complete today,' Magnus adds as he stands on the front steps.

Reaper is hiding in a neighbouring tree, appearing out of place. I'm feeling sorry for him, having been alone for so long and now feeling out of place in a bustling, lush town.

'There's something I need to do before we begin the paperwork,' I tell Magnus.

'Oh?'

I approach the tree where Reaper is hiding. He observes as I grab for a limb and snap a twig. I extend my right arm. Reaper descends from the tree, lands on my arm, and walks up to my shoulder.

'I have a surprise for you, Reaper,' I say.

'A surprise for me?' he says.

'Yes,' I answer as I walk around the packhouse. I raise my hands and form a circle with my thumbs and fingers. Through the circle of my fingers, I stare up to the sky. 'Right here will be perfect,'

'Perfect for what, exactly?' Reaper asks.
'Your new home,' I say, smiling.
Magnus comes over, curious about what I'm doing. Kneeling, I set the twig on the ground, close my eyes, and place my hands on either side of the twig.

'Revitilo Sprouto,' I say. The ground rumbles and the twig grows into the same majestic moon tree in Silverfay forest, complete with two broad bending branches, forming a barren circle in the centre where we can view the moon at night.

Reaper caws, flaps his wings and soars into the tree.
'My tree!' he exclaims.
Magnus puts his arm around my shoulder. 'Does this mean I don't have to be concerned about Reaper staring at me all night?'
'Yep, I think he'll feel more at ease now,' I smile.
Magnus grabs my hand and leads me upstairs to our office, where we begin going over papers together.

By late afternoon, the witches had returned and informed us how much fun they had mending signs, poles, fences, and anything else that needed TLC with their magic.

'The townspeople were ecstatic, and we also got complimentary cupcakes from the baker.' Lilac explains.

'That's fantastic, and I'm sure Yiselda would enjoy hearing everything about it.' I smile.

'We were thinking about paying her a visit tomorrow,' Ria replies.

'She'd love that! Do you think I could come too?' I ask.

'Of course, you're welcome to join us,' Fern adds.

'I'm going to see Pandora's Box tomorrow,' I exclaim to Magnus.

'Should I come as well?' he wonders, concerned.

'We'll see.' I wink.

We all have dinner and then retire to our rooms. I open the window and gaze out at the moon tree. 'Goodnight, Reaper,' I shout.

'Goodnight, Master,' he says, mind-linking.

'You do know you can just call me Nina or Luna?'

'You could call me Reaper instead of Rooster,' he quips.

'Oh, Reaper,' I chuckle. 'Have a wonderful night, okay?'

'Yes, Luna. You have a good sleep as well, and I suppose I hope Magnus has a good sleep too.'

I can't help but smile at his attempt to be friendlier to Magnus.

I leave the window ajar just in case and snuggle into bed with Magnus. The night flew by, and before I knew it, it was morning.

'Luna, people are arriving, but I sense they are not arriving in good faith,' Reaper says as he flies in and pulls the sheet from us.

'Huh?' I get out of bed, toss my feet to the floor, and stroll over to the window. There are three huge Alphas, each with a dozen other wolves. I can barely make out the wolf emblem in the sunshine, blinding me. The wolf council is here.

'Magnus! The Wolf Council has arrived!' Magnus runs to the window and looks out. He rapidly dresses once he realises I'm correct. I put on my pants and a simple tee and slip my wand into my back pocket. Reaper flies out the window in their direction. I find myself seeing through his eyes and hearing what Reaper hears.

Alpha Bennet snarls, 'Alpha Magnus better have a solid justification for this,'

'It might be rumour and not fact. What wolf community would unite with witches?' Alpha Amir says.

'One who has been bewitched,' Alpha Theaton chuckles.

Alpha Bennet growls, 'Not funny. If this is true, it's quite dangerous, and don't forget they killed Alpha Zenith, who used to be a member of our wolf council.'

Alpha Theaton's demeanour shifts from light-hearted to solemn.

I revert to myself and turn to Magnus, 'They've come to see if we have any witches living here. They don't appear pleased with the prospect of it being real,'

'I'm confident that everything will be alright, but I'll mind-link my parents to join us. They might be able to help put the wolf council at ease.'

I nod and proceed downstairs, preparing to face the wolf council.

Chapter 9

When we hear the thunderous thuds, Magnus answers the door, 'What brings us the pleasure of welcoming the Wolf Council?' Magnus chirps.

'Alpha Magnus, we've come to talk about some fairly serious worries that have everyone on edge.' Alpha Bennet says.

'Please come in and join us in the dining room for some refreshments,' Magnus adds as he opens the door wider.

Magnus frowns at the scores of men following them as they enter. 'Perhaps you could all go to the ceremony hall, where there is more room, and I'll get you food and refreshments?' The Alphas signal them to proceed to the ceremonial hall. Magnus was about to close the door when Ryker and Astrid arrived.

'I'm pleased you're here, Mum and Dad,' Magnus says.

'We want to reassure the wolf council that they have nothing to be concerned about.' Ryker explains.

While the kitchen staff brings out beverages and nibbles, we take our seats at the table.

'So, what's this troubling news you've heard that has prompted you to come here?' Magnus inquires.

Alpha Amir and Alpha Theaton wait for Alpha Bennet to speak.

'At first, we heard that your Mate and Luna is supposedly half-witch. We ignored the rumours since we knew they were ridiculous, only to then hear that you have initiated a number of witches into your pack? Now we're all aware that witches haven't existed for hundreds of years, so please explain why the packs continue to believe these rumours are genuine?' he says, resting his hand flat on the table.

Magnus squeezes my hand to reassure me before responding to the Alphas.

'Well, you see, you're hearing all of this because it's true. Nina's grandmother was a witch, and the powers were passed down through her mother's generation. The witches of the Midnight Coven learned about it and requested to live peacefully amongst us. We decided that the witches would be welcome to join us,'

There is a brief pause before the three Alphas burst out laughing.

'Skedaddle Dash,' I hear one of the girls upstairs exclaim. Fern appears in a blink, seated next to us. The Alphas stop laughing and act shocked. Ela, Ria, and Lilac join us at the table, giggling. They ignore the Alphas and continue to converse while the cook serves out a tray of pancakes. Lilac takes half of the stack and places it on her plate, then Ria takes a few, leaving two for Ela to take.

'I would like some as well, you know?' Fern frowns.

Ela smiles and waves her wands over her pancakes and says, 'Spawniate.' Suddenly, her two pancakes have multiplied into a stack of ten. She joyfully claps her hands and sets five onto Fern's plate.

'Thank you, Ela,' Fern says, smiling.

'Would anyone else like some?' Ela inquires, now turning to face the rest of us at the table.

As they observe the four witches eating breakfast, the Alphas have gone quiet and pale.

'Thank you, Ela. We're good for the time being,' I smile. 'I'd like to introduce you to our rather speechless visitors, Alpha Amir, Alpha Bennet, and Alpha Theaton. The wolf council is made up of them.'

The mention of the wolf council has piqued the witches' interest. They pause their eating and smile at the Alphas.

'Hello, my name is Fern,', 'I'm Ria.', 'Lilac, here,' she says. 'Ela, and we're the Midnight Coven,' Ela explains. 'Well, mostly, because Yiselda isn't here,' Ela adds.

'But there haven't been any witches in hundreds of years. So, how did you end up here, and how do you exist?' Alpha Bennet inquires irritably.

'That's because your grandparents' generation nearly wiped us out. Fortunately, a few of us, like Yiselda, survived. We learned that the new Luna of Shadow Crest was half-witch and felt we would be safe here. None of you would be here right now if Yiselda hadn't survived the witch hunt. So it is because of her that the world is safe.' Fern explains.

'Huh! Safe! How can the world be considered safe when you dang witches exist?' Alpha Bennet snarls.

The witches stand up abruptly, now displeased with Alpha Bennet.

'Well, we dang witches have never caused any issues with the werewolf population. It's because you were afraid of our magic, despite the fact that we used it hundreds of years ago to heal your species and help your towns develop and prosper. The alphas grew irritated. Everyone came to us for help instead of them, and they began telling everyone that we were using spells against them. Everything was a lie. If you fully understood the ways of witches, you would understand how pleased it makes us helping others of any species. We never murdered any of your kind unless it was in self-defence or when we had no other option. We were always tranquil, and we still are,' Ela says, fighting back the tears.

'Let's all take a deep breath and relax as we absorb all of this information,' I say.

'Relax? While there are witches present?' Alpha Theaton scoffs.

Magnus slams his fist against the table, drawing everyone's attention to himself.

'You forget my Mate, and the Luna of this pack is a witch. Even if you are the Wolf council, you will show respect while in my territory and will not speak ill of the Luna or other witches. Whether you like it or not, Fern, Lilac, Ria, and

Ela are now members of this pack, and they will be treated respectfully as equals.'

Magnus receives a proud nod from Ryker.

'Alpha Magnus, my son, is correct. Our pack welcomed them all with open arms. They are now part of our family,' Ryker says, backing up his son's choice.

'Ever since your Mate Astrid murdered our fellow councilor, Alpha Zenith, we've all suspected that this pack will be a problem in the future. Speaking of the apple falling far from the tree, we hear Alpha Magnus is also to blame for his grandson's death, Moss?' Alpha Bennet fires back.

Astrid's hands are trembling. With the past being brought up, I can sense she is in anguish. I reach out and take her hand in mine. She offers me a grateful expression.

'Alpha Zenith kidnapped Astrid and planned to force her to mate with his son. Moss followed in his footsteps and kidnapped Nina, intending to force her to be his Mate. Their killings were justified, and they had no one to blame except themselves.' Ryker retorts.

Alpha Bennet taps his fingers on the table repeatedly in thought. Finally, he stands up and steps forward, rubbing his chin.

'Now that we've established the rumours are true, Alpha Amir, Alpha Theaton, and I have a lot to talk about concerning this problem,' says Alpha Amir.

'But there isn't a problem,' Magnus asserts firmly.

'Perhaps it isn't a problem in your eyes because they are in your pack. As a result, they may be utilised against other packs.' Alpha Bennet mutters.

'Did you not hear a word we said?' Ela snaps. 'We simply told you we were peaceful. We weren't the ones going about annihilating werewolves,'

'But you did claim you killed some a few moments ago,' he counters.

'Because they were about to kill us even though we had done nothing wrong! You don't understand, do you? You have no idea how important it is for witches to live. Without witches, you would all perish, humans included!' Ela yells.

The alphas of the wolf council burst out laughing. 'Well, for the previous hundreds of years or so, we've seemed to do just well without you,' Alpha Theaton exclaims.

'That's because we've been in hiding to ensure your survival, including the human species, by keeping all your greatest nightmares locked up with spells in Pandora's Box, you morons,' Fern exclaims.

They stop laughing, their demeanour shifts, and they lock their gaze on Fern.

'I believe it would be in your best advantage to tell us more about this Pandora's Box,' Alpha Amir suggests.

Chapter 10

'Ironically, I think it's in your best interests to know what we're doing to save this world from being destroyed, and maybe, by some miracle, you'll come to some type of mutual respect for us witches,' Fern says. 'It has been entrusted upon Yiselda for the previous two hundred years to take over Pandora's Box and stay there. It was known as the Midnight Covenstead for generations until the Vampire King sought revenge on the humans for the death of his blood flame.

He summoned Shadow Reapers and Grimghouls and released them into the world. As a result, many werewolves were killed, and their territories were seized. It was only a matter of time before they infiltrated human settlements, and as you know, humans must never learn about the supernatural side of our world.

Many witches banded together and used their power. We were able to imprison the Vampire King and his minions inside the Midnight Covenstead, where spells were put to keep them locked up for good.

Centuries had passed, and the witches and wolves had coexisted peacefully until the Alphas were dissatisfied with the love and adoration, we got from their pack members. They lied to their pack, claiming they were cursed and that all witches must be slain, so we can't control them with spells. As a result, they set out to find us. It was the largest witch hunt in history.

Yiselda was the only survivor of the Midnight Coven after the witch hunt. She remained there, keeping the charms and spells in place, knowing it was now her responsibility to keep the world safe. Years later, in a human village, she stumbled upon us at an orphanage and sensed right away that we weren't humans. We were too little at the time and didn't know we were witches till she brought us in. Since then, she has served as our mother, teacher, and protector. She remains at Pandora's Box to this day in order to protect us all.' Fern explains.

'Do you think we're going to believe that? A Vampire King, Shadow Reapers, or Grimghouls have never existed. Everyone is aware of the past. Witches used their magic against us for selfish reasons, which is why you were wiped out, Alpha Bennet sneers.

'That is completely false!' Fern yells.

Alpha Bennet stands, 'We will take our leave to discuss this, and we will return tomorrow with our decision,'

'What decision? There isn't anything to decide,' Magnus growls.

'The decision on whether or not to allow the witches to reside here or be exiled,' Alpha Bennet smirks, turns, and goes out the door, followed by Alpha Amir and Alpha Theaton before they all leave.

Alpha Amir comes to a halt and turns. 'In the meantime, we'll leave a dozen of our warriors here to keep an eye on the pack until we return tomorrow,' he smiles.

‘They can’t be serious?’ Fern is concerned.

‘You and your sisters are part of this pack. We won’t allow them to harm you, any of you.’ Magnus says.

Reaper flies towards the Alphas, swooping them and then flying back up.

'What in the world was that?' Alpha Bennet says, his head tilted.

'I'm not sure. All I saw was black mist,' says Alpha Theaton.

'Witchcraft, perhaps?' Alpha Amir says, returning his gaze to the packhouse.

Reaper caws and charges at them once more. This time, they come across a big black raven. They run from our territory, escaping Reaper.

Reaper flies inside the house and lands on my shoulder.

‘Reaper chasing after them off isn’t going to help our situation,’ I say to him.

He mind-links, ‘It doesn’t matter what we do. They have a vendetta against this pack,’

'Do you really think so?'

'They had already decided they didn't like witches before they stepped foot in this packhouse. When they return tomorrow, it will not be with good news,' Reaper mind-links.

'We should probably see Yiselda,' Fern says. They all nod and walk outside. Ela redraws a star within a circle on the ground while Ria places the stones at each point.

'Just step into the circle, and it will teleport you there with us.' Lilac explains.

As soon as they all step in and teleport, I follow and instantly appear in front of Pandora's box, surrounded by a dense forest. The Covenstead has a red tint, and any framework and lattice around it is a dark brown. The chimney is emitting smoke, and a window shutter swings open.

Ria yells, 'Come on, Luna, the entrance is this way.'

I accompany them inside the Covenstead. I'm dizzy from spinning around since there's so much going on. On the bookshelf, books and knick-knacks are rearranging themselves. A broom is sweeping the floor on its own. There are cats, frogs, spiders, and even a chicken roaming the area. We follow the sound of bubbling water into the kitchen. I expected to see a kitchen island instead of a large black cauldron. Steam and bubbles float to the surface, and I cringe when I discover the bubbling fluid is green.

'I'm so delighted you all came to visit,' Yiselda smiles. We all crowd around and share one giant hug. 'Let me put the kettle on, and we'll have some tea while you girls tell me how well you're settling into Shadow Crest,' she says. Yiselda turns and wields her wand, saying, 'Lifto Levitatous, Aqua Bedew, Inferno Flamo.'

We watch as a black iron kettle floats over to the tap, fills with water, and then floats over to the fire, hovering over it.

She waves her wand again, this time at a teacup and saucer, saying, 'Lifto Levitatous.' The cup and saucer drift to the dining table and land. She says, 'Spawniate.' The cup and saucer multiply to become a set of six on the table.

'Lifto Levitatous,' she says as she calls the pot of water over to the table. The kettle floats and tips over, dumping boiling water into our teacups. I place a tea bag on the saucer after dipping it in my teacup until I'm satisfied with the strength.

Yiselda has come to join us at the table. 'How has it been so far?' she inquires.

'We had a lot of fun, went into town, met many people, and even got free cupcakes from the baker when we helped replace the broken fence and sign,' Lilac says.

'They were very thankful,' Ria smiles.

'I'm delighted to hear everything is going well,' Yiselda says.

'Well, until today, when the wolf council came to visit us,' Fern explains.

Yiselda almost spills her tea as she stares at me.

'Unfortunately, they don't appreciate the fact that we've let witches into our pack. They believe witches used to cast spells against them, which is why their predecessors fought against witches,'

Yiselda sighs, placing her teacup on the saucer.

'It's a shame their parents and grandparents have lied to them about us. They don't plan on causing any harm to the girls, do they?' She asks me.

'Well, they left not in the greatest mood to discuss the matter. The wolf council said they would return tomorrow with their verdict. Magnus insisted us witches are not a problem and that the girls had already been initiated and welcomed. Alpha Bennet claimed we could turn against them using the witches to our advantage. I'm hoping they come to their senses and understand witches just want to help,' I say.

'We even told them they needed us because of Pandora's Box, but they didn't seem to believe me when I told them why,' Fern says.

'If something happens to any of you, or if you believe you are in danger, please return here immediately, okay?'

'Yes, Yiselda,' they all say at the same time.

Chapter 11

The chicken walks into the kitchen and pecks at random crumbs on the floor.

'This place is incredible. Do you think I could get a tour?' I ask Yiselda.

'Of course, as a Midnight Coven member, this is also your home now,' she says proudly. She leads us down a lengthy corridor. I'm perplexed because even though the Covenstead appeared to be quite significant from the outside, this hall seems to be at least still twice the outside length. As we proceed down the corridor, I notice that there are no doors, only old picture paintings of witches who were members of the midnight coven until they died or were killed. I come to a halt in front of one to observe its beauty more thoroughly. I take a step back. As the artwork moves, I leap back and scream. The witch in the portrait briefly bends her head and smiles before returning to her previous stance.

'Luna, what is it?' Lilac asks, concerned, as she places a hand on my shoulder. I point to the portrait.

'She moved,' I said.

'Oh, yeah, they all do that,' She shrugs.

'You could have given me a heads up?' I grumble.

'Luna, we're in Pandora's Box, silly. You should expect anything here, from your brightest dreams to your worst nightmares,' she giggles.

I roll my eyes and proceed to follow the others. When we reach the end of the corridor, there is no door, only a mirror. I glance at the reflection of all of us, confused.

'Are there no doors? This is simply a mirror,' I say.

Yiselda and the other smile and walk through the mirror. It ripples like water as they walk through it. I reach my hand out and quickly poke it with my finger—the mirror ripples. In astonishment, I then put my entire hand through. Someone on the other side takes my hand and pulls me through.

‘Hurry up, slowpoke,’ Ria laughs.

Yiselda leads us along an irregularly shaped corridor with three doors, one in front of me, one on the left, and one on the right.
'The sleeping quarters are via this door on the left.'

I follow her through the door and into a corridor with ten doors.
'These are all bedrooms,' she says as she opens the closest door.
The bed is a big mattress that floats above the floor, with silk bedding dangling from the sides. Furniture moves around the room as though it has its own mind. Candles float above the bed, softly lighting the space.

'All right, then,' I answer, knowing this is out of the ordinary but not knowing what to say. A mahogany French wardrobe comes to a halt and faces me. I'm not sure if I should say hello. Magnus will think I'm insane if I start talking to furniture. Instead, I walked out of the room cautiously.

The others join me, and we make our way back to the corridor with the three doors.

'This middle door leads to the library, and another door in the library leads to the enchanted garden,' adds Yiselda.

We walk into the library. There's a beautiful globe of the world. I spin it carefully and appreciate it. There are a few little tables where we can read. As I approach certain books, I notice that they are quite old. 'Book of spells, Book of potions, Book of magic, Book of wards,' I read various titles.

At the back of the library, there are two double doors. Fern opens them, and my mouth drops open in awe at the beauty. Like fairies, there are small balls of light floating around. I chuckle as I see the cutest garden gnome statues, some with their bellies hanging out. I've never seen such lush trees and a colourful abundance of flowers. Toadstools, some of which were taller than me. I come to a halt as I notice something white moving beyond the bushes.

'Is that a horse?' I ask.

Everyone laughs as Fern responds, 'No, Luna, it's a unicorn.'

I laugh this time until the horse steps forwards, a horn illuminating a white glow on its head.

‘Wait! 'It's a unicorn!' I say this while pointing at it. 'I thought you were joking?'

'No, I was serious,' Fern says, laughing.

'This place is incredible. I can't believe you've got a unicorn here!'

I stroke and pat the unicorn softly. 'She is lovely,' I say.

Yiselda remarks. 'Her name is Star.'

'Hello, my name is Nina,' I smile. Star gently rubs her head on my face.

I look over at the garden gnomes and kneel in front of the one with the red cap and green shirt with its belly hanging out. My face is millimetres away from his.

'I swear he had his hands on his hips, and now he's waving his hand?'

The gnome suddenly leans forwards, snatches a kiss off my lips, and smiles. My cheeks flush.

'You, you tiny gnome! You can't simply steal a kiss like that! 'I'm mates with Alpha Magnus,' I growl. Snickering, the chubby gnome turns and rushes into the bushes.

The witches are trying hard not to laugh.

'It's time to see the rest of Pandora's Box,' says Yiselda.

We walk out of the library and into the hallway with the three doors.

'Now, the door on your right is one you should never enter on your own. The Vampire King and his minions are held under spell and ward in the dungeon.'

When the door opens, there is nothing but darkness. There doesn't appear to be a floor.

Yiselda says, 'Materialise,' and a book emerges in her hand. She sets it at the foot of the door on the ground. 'Sprouto Spawniate,' she says, casting.

The book expands five times in size, then multiplies and stacks up, forming a staircase made from books.

'Wow, that was cool,' I say. Yiselda beams.

Everyone takes their wands and flicks the tip, sparking a heatless flame that illuminates the dark stairs. They make their way up the steps. I grab my wand, flick it for light, and proceed up the stairs. Inside is a black wooden door with a white circle containing sigils.

'These sigils you see are wards designed to prevent the Vampire King from fleeing. You never, ever, ever wipe them away.' Yiselda states sternly. I nod.

We enter the dungeon once she opens the entrance. It's gloomy and dark. I can hear a variety of threatening noises. Shrills, moans, growls, and hisses. Many cell doors have little green and grey hands reaching out to me. I'm struck by how long their claws are. When I get closer and see countless little goblin creatures with razor-sharp fangs snapping and gnarling, I gasp and cover my mouth. They try to reach deeper through the bars with their long dirty claws to grab me. They're various shades of green and grey, with black eyes, and I know I'm looking at some of the most frightening creatures I've ever seen.

'Grimghouls,' Ela says. 'They're horrible little things. They have razor-sharp teeth and can rip anyone to shreds in seconds. They have a hunger for flesh,' she explains.

The concept makes me shudder. We proceed deeper into the dungeon. When I gaze into the cells, I notice that the darkness moves.

'How come it appears that something is in there, yet no one is in there?' I ask.

'Shadow Reapers,' Ela calls them. 'They are shadow entities; they hide in the shadows, so you don't notice them. They take control of your mind and body. They make you see things that aren't there. They are hallucinogens that cause you to perform crazy things, typically leading to your death or the killing of others,'

I back up a few steps.

'Yeah, no thanks.' I say, frowning.

Chapter 12

A strange but warm sense overcomes me. I look to the darkness ahead, noticing crimson eyes staring right at me, flickering like a flame. My body feels drawn toward him, and my mind feels like it's going a hundred miles per hour. My wand glows brightly enough to see two hands grasping the bars as I approach, his eyes still fixed on me.

I suddenly hear a husky whisper in my mind. 'This way, come closer. It's okay, come to me,' the voice says.

Without realising it, my hand stretches out to touch him. He grips my wrist gently, and I feel a slight burn on my wrist. Yiselda grabs my arm and pulls me back.

'Be careful dear, that is the Vampire King, Alec,' she warns. Then, raising her wand, his cell lights up. I glimpse his dark hair and light brown eyes before he flourishes his cloak over his face and retreats to the far corner.

I examine my wrist and notice a peculiar mark. A strange sensation runs through my body. I shake it off and turn to face Alec.

He lowers his cloak slightly enough to peer at me. He is very handsome. He looks at Yiselda.

‘Could you at least dim that darn light, Yiselda?’ he sneers.

‘Dimulous,’ she says, and her wand dims low.

Alec lowers his cloak and floats forward. ‘You’re so beautiful. How I would love to taste your blood. I have a feeling it would taste sweeter than honey,’ he smiles, licking his lips and revealing his fangs.

'Well, lucky for me, King Alec, you're imprisoned behind these bars. I also don’t plan to be on your menu. Sorry, you won’t get to take a bite,' I grin.

He gives me a curious look for a few moments.

'I don't intend to stay in here indefinitely, Nina,' his demeanour softening.

'How did you figure out my name?' I ask, stroking the blemish on my wrist. It has a peculiar warmth about it.

'I am Alec! Vampire King, I can figure out a lot by being in your presence, and I may have overheard one of the other witches call you that,' he admits.

I try not to laugh at his honesty. He smiles sweetly at me and looks over my shoulder.

'Yiselda, we have a new guest. How about you let me out so I can give Nina here a proper warm welcome,' he says sincerely.

Yiselda laughs, 'Yeah, right, I'm going to let you out so you can flee and wreak havoc across the world until everyone bows to you and declares you ruler of the world,' she scoffs.

'Why not? It sounds like lots of fun to me,' he says.

'Except it's not pleasant for everyone who dies as a result,' Yiselda argues.

'Those nasty humans deserve to die for what they did to me all those years ago,' King Alec growls. 'My Juniper, my darling, sweet Juniper,' he murmurs as he withdraws into the shadows. As I hear him sob, I frown and feel sorry for him. I have no idea who Juniper is or what happened to her, but I can sense what he's going through. My heart hurts and feels as if it were a shattered glass that can't be repaired. My inner self seems gloomy and empty all of a sudden. I place my hand on my chest.

‘Luna, are you alright?’ Yiselda asks. I nod my head.

‘I’m fine, just a little overwhelmed with Pandora’s Box and its contents,’ I joke.

‘Well, now that the formalities are over and done with and the tour is complete, we shall return downstairs,’ Yiselda says, turning away. I go to follow her.

‘Wait!’ Reaching out between the bars, King Alec touches my arm with his fingers. He can't grasp me because I'm too far away. From where his fingers brushed against me, I feel a warm sense of sparks. I examine my arm, and it feels as if Magnus himself has touched me. When I look up, I notice King Alec's warm smile.

'Until we meet again, just don't make me wait too long, my Queen,' he whispers, so only I hear.

I take a few steps backwards with a worried expression on my face. Fern grabs my hand and drags me behind her as she skips toward the exit. I keep returning my eyes to King Alec, and his focus does not leave me until we reach the opposite end of the dungeon and depart.

Yiselda closes the door with the ward spell. As we travel down the stairwell of books, we return to the kitchen by entering the corridor and walking through the other door, which happens to be the large mirror.

Yiselda, using her magic, pours us another cup of tea as they converse and laugh. But I'm not sure what it's about since I can't stop thinking about King Alec. I shake my head and think about Magnus instead. I want to be in his arms, and I need to get rid of these strange feelings.

'It's been wonderful seeing you, Yiselda, but it's time for us to return to Shadow Crest. Will you be accompanying us when the wolf council returns tomorrow?' I ask.

'It's probably better if I'm there, just in case.' She answers.

I follow Fern, Ria, Ela and Lilac past the chicken, cats, frogs, floating objects and the broom sweeping the entrance again and out the door. There is a permanently drawn circle with a star and stones inside. We all step in one by one. I think of home and Magnus as I step in. When I open my eyes, we appear near the bonfire. Reaper caws from his moon tree as I run inside the packhouse, up the stairs and into the office, where I wrap my arms around Magnus and kiss him.

'Welcome back,' he says, 'How was it?'

'You should have seen the place. It was more than I imagined it to be. There were strangely shaped hallways, a broom sweeping by itself. They even had a unicorn in the enchanted garden!'

'A unicorn?'

'Yep, her name is Star,' I smile.

'So, what about those Grim things and nightmarish creatures Yiselda mentioned?'

I take my wrist in my hands and begin caressing the mark on it.

'The Grimghouls were terrifying small creatures with razor-sharp teeth. On the other hand, the Shadow Reapers were difficult to spot since they resembled shadows, shaped like people. They can fuse with your body, causing you to have hallucinations and harm others,'

'They sound awful?' Magnus says.

'They were, then there was Alec, the Vampire King.' I say, pulling my wrist into my chest.

Magnus takes my hand, extends my arm, and peers at my wrists.

'How long have you had this tattoo? It looks like an Ankh? Like a sword with a circle around the grip, like a symbol?' he asks.

I examine my wrist once more, the redness and discomfort have subsided, and I can now see what Magnus sees. It does resemble an Ankh in appearance.

'I'm not sure. Alec grabbed me and-,'

'He did what?' Magnus growls, abruptly standing up. 'He did this to you?'

'I-I don't know. It happened so quickly. When he grabbed me, I felt a slight burn on my wrist. Then I felt strange and left as soon as I could,'

'I'll take you to the pack doctor,'

'Magnus, it's fine. It doesn't hurt anymore, and I feel fine now that I'm here with you,' I assure him.

He relaxes a little.

'Fine, but if you feel strange again or any pain, you let me know, okay?' he says.

I nod, and he places a kiss on my forehead.

'Good girl.' He smiles.

Chapter 13

Reaper caws and taps his beak on the window. 'Next time, you need to take me with you, Luna. You can't just leave your familiar behind. It's dangerous,' Reaper mind-links.

'The other witches didn't take their familiars with them. So, I don't see what the big deal is?'

'It's a big deal, now let me inside… please,'

I open the window, and he flies toward me. He calms the moment he lands on my shoulder. His beak is pressed against my nose as I turn my face, and his eyes stare into mine.

'Reaper, what the heck?' I say.

'There is something different about you. Did something happen at Pandora's Box?'

'No Reaper, nothing happened,' I frown.

'I thought I sensed something odd whilst you were in Pandora's Box. I was worried something had happened to you?'

'Reaper, nothing happened. Let's take a walk outside.' Ela's toad leaps down the front steps as I open the front door, 'I need some fresh air.' The witches are conversing beneath Reaper's moon tree. Ria's snake is dangling from a branch above them.

I take a deep breath and take in the tranquil surroundings. My wrist tingles, but I ignore it on purpose.

'I'm heading to the lake for a swim. Would you all like to come along with me?' I ask.

'Next time, Luna,' Ria says with a smile.

'All right,' I remark as I walk towards the lake.

I remove my clothes and dive into the lake. Reaper perches on a nearby tree. Closing my eyes, I float on my back. Flashbacks of King Alec grabbing hold of my wrist, the subtle burn on my wrist imprinted into an ankh. His crimson eyes changed into a light brown. His gaze, the way he looked at me. I should have been afraid to be in his presence, but I wasn't. If anything, I don't think I wanted to leave, but why do I feel comfortable around him?

I finished my swim, dried off and returned to the packhouse. Reaper flew high in the air and followed me.

The witches are no longer under the moon tree, but the packhouse emits various scents. Fern's cat purrs as he brushes against my leg. I walk into the home and head downstairs to the basement, following the different aromas.

Herbs are hung on the walls, and jars are stacked on the shelves. I'm not sure what's in them, but I have a feeling I don't want to find out. Ria, Fern, Lilac, May, and Ela add ingredients to a massive bubbling cauldron.

May waggles her finger at me, then mutters, 'I wish I could have gone to Pandora's Box as well,'

'Next time,' I say with a smile to May.

'Can you make a promise?' she asks.

Ela assures her, 'We all promise,'

'How did you get all of this?' I ask them.

Fern grins, 'Oh, we just used the Materialise spell,'

'Can you explain how that spell works? Isn't that the magic Yiselda used to summon a book?'

'That's right, and it's that simple. All you have to do is imagine the item you want. I'll demonstrate.

Let's pretend I'm hungry for a cherry pie. So I wave my wand and say, "Materialise," picturing a cherry pie.'

Suddenly In her palm, the pie appears. She holds a pie that smells like cooked cherries. 'Ouch,' she exclaims as she tosses it on the table.

She laughs, 'I probably should have thought of a cold cherry pie,' We're all laughing. 'Now you try,' she says.

'Alright,' I think of a rose so perfect. It has no blemishes or broken petals. 'Materialise,' I say and open my eyes to see I'm holding the rose I envisioned.

'Ooh, pretty,' Lilac says.

'So, what exactly are you guys doing here?'

'We're conjuring up potions!' Ria beams.

'Can I help?' I ask excitedly. Reaper caws, 'I think Reaper wants to help too?'

'Sure!' Ela says.

'What potion are you currently making?'

Ela walks me over to a table and points to an open book.

'Hey, that's my book. Magnus, let me keep it from the library,' I frown.

'Oh, sorry, we saw it on the shelf in the living room and thought no one would mind if we borrowed it?'

'I suppose it's okay, Ela. Just be gentle with it.'

'Yay!' she squeals and hugs me.

I look to the open page and read it out.

'Elixir of healing:
Over bubbling water, add
Five drops of mermaid tears
A snippet of unicorn hair
The bark of the Willow
Sprig of Thyme
Incantation:
With these wounds that thee feel,
remove the pain and make thee heal
If unwell, don't let it dwell,
use this spell to make thee well.'

'We just need to add the Thyme, Luna. Could you please bring a sprig to the cauldron?' Ela asks.

'Sure,' I say as I walk over to the wall where the various herbal sprigs are tied up in bundles. The smells are pleasant, and I can't help but smile. Then, taking a sprig of thyme, I pass it to Reaper, who flies over the cauldron and drops it into the bubbling water.

Fern starts stirring it with a wooden ladle.

Let's recite the chant together, says Fern.

'With these wounds that thee feel,
remove the pain and make thee heal
If unwell, don't let it dwell,
use this spell to make thee well.' We all say.
The cauldron releases a plume of green smoke.
Fern grins as she says, 'It's done, now to bottle it.'

May and I assist in filling the vials with the healing potion and cork-sealing the vials. Ela then prepares the labels, Ria writes on them, and Lilac and I stick them on the vials and carefully position them on a shelf.

'Perhaps we might concoct an elixir of love, fertility, or strength tomorrow?' Ela says.
'I was thinking the elixir of resistance?' Fern replies.
'With your snoring, Fern, I thought maybe the elixir of sleep?' Lilac says.
We all laugh as poor Fern frowns.

Chapter 14

I'm wrapped in Magnus's arms when I wake up.

'Please tell me today isn't today?' he murmurs.

'All right, Magnus, today isn't today,' I grin.

'Er, it's really today, isn't it?'

'The day the wolf council's three-boofhead alphas return to tell us whether they support or oppose the witches staying here and what they plan to do if they oppose it?' I say.

'Yeah… that day.'

'Look, I'm sure they've come to their senses and realised that allowing witches into our pack is wonderful now that they've had some time to think about it,' I reassure him.

'I guess I'll spend the day with your father to see if our warriors are prepared as a precautionary measure,' he says.

'Sure, I'll spend the day in the basement with the other witches until the wolf council arrives.'

Immediately after breakfast, the witches head downstairs.

'Can I come to watch you all make potions?' Josie asks.

'Sure,' I smile. May and Josie walk with me down to the basement.

'So, have we figured out what potion we are making today?' I smile.

Everyone shakes their heads no.

'We couldn't agree on one,' Fern says.

I walk over to my book of potions and flick through the pages.

'Resistance to heat, Resistance to the cold, breathe underwater, Swiftness, Deadly nightshade, Wolfsbane, Elixir of Truth, Elixir of Fire, fertility, Ooh elixir of the dead sounds interesting?' I say.

Fern, Ria, Ela and Lilac all gasp.

'Luna, you can't choose the elixir of the dead. It's far too dangerous,' Fern warns.

'Fern is correct. Drinking the potion allows you to see ghosts, and poltergeists can injure you if you encounter one,' Ela explains.

'Oh, well, how about we practice some new spells then?' I say, placing the book of potions down. Suddenly an idea hits me. 'We should all go the town library to the forbidden room,' I say, pulling the key up from around my neck.

'What's in the forbidden room?' Lilac asks.

'Spellbooks and lots of them and other interesting items that must be hundreds of years old.'

Everyone looks at each other with a nod and smiles.

'Let's go,' Ria says.

We arrive at the library. I lead them to the back room with the locked door and use my key to open it. Then, pulling my wand out, I flick the tip, and it lights up. Fern and Ela flick their wands up too, 'Illuminate,' I say, lighting up the whole room.

'Woah!' They all say. 'Luna, do you even know what this room is?' Fern asks.

'Yeah, it's the forbidden room. It's been locked for hundreds of years, so no one could access any of the books as magic was never allowed,'

'Luna, this room isn't just to lock books away. This table isn't just a table. It's an altar. This room is a secret witches' study and an ancient one,'

'Ooh, really?'

'I believe Fern is correct. Take a look at all of this, and these volumes are centuries-old.' Ela replies as she rolls one of the scrolls out onto the alter, 'Even these scrolls appear ancient. This is a gateway spell to access the Realm of Shadows,' she exclaims. 'It's the home of the vampires. It's also where Alec, the Vampire King, has his fortress,'

'These aren't ordinary spells, Luna,' Lilac says as she reads the titles on the other scrolls, 'No witch, wizard, or mage even knows how to cast half of what's in this room.'

There is a burlap sack in the corner of the room hanging from the handle of an old broom made from a branch—the bristles are made from sticks. I take the burlap sack over my shoulder and place a couple of books and as many scrolls as possible carefully inside the bag.

'We should bring some books back home with us,' I say.

'Luna, there are a lot of spells in here that are quite harmful. Maybe we should leave them? They are locked in here for a reason,' Ela says.

'Ela is right,' Reaper mind-links.

I take the scroll Ela had rolled out on the alter, tie the red ribbon around it, and place it back on the shelf.

'It's fine. I'll just take a couple of books to read,' I reassure them all.

I take the gleaming athame with the black handle and silver inscriptions, and they grimace at each other. The knife has a blue gem at the bottom, and the blade is silver at first, then purple, and finally black at the tip. There is a black leather sheath near it. I place it in the sheath and tuck it into my belt.

Reaper flies over my shoulder and snatches a book from one of the bookcases. Then he flies back over to me, drops it in my hands, and lands on my shoulder again.

'If you're going to start collecting magical weapons, you need to learn about them at the very least to keep yourself safe.' Mind-links Reaper, I fix my gaze on the book I'm holding.

I read aloud, 'A guide for magical weapons,' then nod at Reaper and stuff it into my burlap bag.

I grab the Quill sitting in a vat of black ink, go to the bear corner of the room, and draw a circle with a star inside. 'No stones…' I think with my hands on my hips and look at the old stone wall with small crumbling parts. I collect five crumpled rocks and place them at the tip of each star point.

'There, now we have a permanent port to get here,' I smile. 'Let's go back home. Yiselda and the wolf council will be arriving soon.'

I step into the circle, thinking of home and appear by the bonfire. The others appear behind me, and we return to the packhouse.

Instead of joining the girls upstairs, I go to my room, sit on my bed, and open the burlap bag. I place the book on weaponry beside me and pick the next book up. 'Mysteria: The history of supernaturals,' I read aloud, looking forward to reading this book. I place it down and start reading the book on weaponry first. Reaper sits on the balcony edge and looks out.

My mind wanders back to Alec, and for some reason, I want to see him again. 'Don't be so ridiculous, Nina,' I say. Reaper turns to stare at me.

'Did you know that talking to oneself is a classic sign of insanity?' Reaper mind-links.

'Yeah, yeah,' I say, waving my hand towards him. 'I probably am insane?'

'Why would you think that?' He asks.

'When I'm not thinking of Magnus, I'm thinking of the Vampire King. There has to be something wrong with me?' I reasoned.

Reaper gazes at me silently as if analyzing me, and the silent staring starts to creep me out, so I return my focus to the book of weaponry.

There are odd-shaped staffs with various gem forms atop them, wands with multiple patterns and jewels, Chakrams, charms, and jewelry. Finally, I've progressed to knives and athames. I scroll through the pages and find the identical athame I had discovered in the forbidden room. Magnus has come home before I get an opportunity to read it.

'Nina?' he says. I put the book down, put it back in my bag, and dash downstairs. Reaper follows. I leap into Magnus's arms and kiss him on the lips. Electrifying sparks fly through my body every time he touches me, and I can't get enough of him. He cradles my face in his hands. He says.

'I love you,'

'I love you, too,' I smile.

Chapter 15

'Let's see what the wolf council has to say. I'm sure they'll be here in a minute.'

A knock comes at the door. We proceed to answer it, expecting to be confronted by the Wolf Council.

'Yiselda,' I draw her in for a hug.

'Did I make it to the meeting on time?' she asks.

'You have,' I say.

'The wolf council hasn't come yet, but they'll be here soon,' Magnus says.

'The others are in the basement. I'll bring them up for the meeting,' I say as I dash downstairs.

'Yiselda has arrived, and the wolf council is on its way,' I notify the witches. They nod and walk upstairs to the dining room, where they hug Yiselda and take their seats.

Reaper warns me that the wolf council is approaching just as Ryker, Astrid, and Leon enter and join us at the table. We all appear nervous.

My mind manifests into Reapers, allowing me to see through his eyes and hear anything he hears. He is perched in the moon tree, looking off towards the distance, where we see the wolf Council approach.

'They're here,' I say to everyone at the table.

'How do you know? No one has knocked?' Magnus says.

'Reaper is showing me through his eyes. They are less than a minute away,' I say.

Within the minute, loud thumps at the door are heard. Magnus greets them and escorts them into the dining room. They sit with serious, stern looks on their faces.

'Alpha, Bennet, Alpha Theaton and Alpha Amir, I would like you to meet Yiselda,' he introduces.

They merely nod without saying anything.

'It's a pleasure to meet you, Alphas of the Wolf Council,' Yiselda replies politely.

'Are you the one who guards Pandora's Box?' Alpha Bennet casts a sly smile.

'That's me,' Yiselda confirms.

'So, what your coven said about it is true?' He asks.

She answers, 'Yes, my coven sisters have no reason to lie,'

'So, you're telling me that a vampire king and other dangerous monsters exist?'

'Correct,'

The Alphas exchange glances as if they are mind-linking.

'Show us,' Alpha Bennet says.

'I'm sorry, but I cannot just let anyone into Pandora's Box. It's a dangerous place. If any spells or wards were to be damaged or removed, the world would be at peril for all of us,' Yiselda explains.

'You let the Luna of Shadow Crest in to see it yesterday,' Alpha Bennet states.

I wondered how they would know that but remembered they left some of their warriors here to watch us.

'Yes, but that's because she's a Midnight Coven member, and it's her responsibility, along with the rest of my sisters, to know all there is to know about Pandora's Box in case anything happens to me,' Yiselda explains.

'How can we be certain these monsters and the vampire king exist?' Alpha Amir asks.

'I suppose you'll never know for sure. You'll just have to take our word for it,' Yiselda replies.

The Alphas laugh bitterly. 'We concluded that without proof of this Pandora's Box and what you are purportedly safeguarding us and the rest of the world from, gives us no option but to banish and exile you witches, and refusal to leave would result in your deaths,' Alpha Bennet sneers.

We all gasp.

'Are you serious, Alpha Bennet?' Magnus shouts.

'I'm very serious, Alpha Magnus, and because your little mate and her sister are half-witches. This new law also includes them,' he states.

Ryker gets out of his chair and steps toward the Alphas.

'You must reconsider. An Alpha needs his Luna. Without them, they are weakened, and you already know that. The witches have caused no harm, and we insist they stay,'

'Sure, they can stay, but we will return with other Alphas and warm the witches upon a fire,' he smiles.

'You can't be seriously thinking about burning them at the stake? They are just young women who want to help us,' I yell at the Alphas.

Alpha Bennet glares at me, 'Mark my word, Luna, if you do not leave, we will make sure you are the first we burn at the stake.' He warns.

Everyone stands up. I pull my wand out along with the other witches while everyone else exposes their morphed canine teeth, ready to shift into their wolves.

‘I suggest you all sit down, put down your wands, and control your wolves,’ Alpha Theaton shouts. ‘We have our legion of warriors on standby if you attack us. They are to destroy this entire pack and wipe you out if you fight,’

‘Are you saying we are not allowed to defend ourselves?’ Magnus yells back.

The Alpha’s laughed, ‘Seems like you are doomed if you do, doomed if you don’t. There won't be a problem as long as the witches leave,’ Alpha Bennet says. ‘You refuse to take us to Pandora’s Box therefore, you have twenty-four hours to rid your territory of any witches. After that, any we find will be killed, and you will be charged for treason resulting in your entire pack being wiped out as punishment.’

They depart abruptly, and we are all stunned, silent, and worried.

‘What are we going to do? I don’t want to leave you, Magnus,’ I say.

'At least until the wolf council changes their minds, we can return to the Covenstead? We don't want to see any harm happen to your pack due to our presence,' Ela says, now upset.

'But I can't leave Magnus, he is my mate, and I can't leave my pack. They rely on me to help run this pack with Magnus,'

Magnus comforts me by wrapping his arms around me and holding me firmly.

'This leaves us with two choices,' Magnus says and looks at Yiselda. 'We have to either take them to Pandora's Box and show them, or we fight them to the death? They will bring many packs with them and overtake us. So the only option without anyone being harmed is to show them the vampire king and his minions,' Magnus says.

Yiselda shakes her head rapidly, 'Magnus, one slip up at Pandora's Box, then it's not just your pack in danger but the whole world. It's a risk I cannot take,'

'It's a risk we must take, Yiselda,' he growls.

Yiselda and Magnus stare as if reading each other's minds even though they cannot.

Yiselda lets out a sigh of defeat, 'I will allow one and only one of the Alphas into Pandora's Box. Alpha Bennet seems to hold the most authority, so it must be him we show. As a precaution, all the witches will accompany us, just in case he tries to do anything stupid while we are there,'

'Done, Leon, chase them down and inform them,' Magnus orders.

'Wait, I have a quicker way,' I grab a pen and piece of paper. I write, Alpha Bennet, Yiselda has agreed to take you and, as a precaution, only you into Pandora's Box tomorrow. Please cease any attack plans until you can see that the witches truly protect all of us, including you. I sign my name and status and whistle for Reaper. He flies towards me. I roll the note up, and he grabs it in his beak.

'Give this note to Alpha Bennet immediately,' I mind-link him. He nods and flies out the window. My mind transmits to Reapers again as he soars above the wolf council. They halt in amazement at the black mist emanating from Reaper's feathers as he soars lower and circles them. Alpha Bennet discovers the rolled-up parchment and snatches it from Reaper, unrolling it. Reaper flies into a nearby tree and keeps an eye on them.

Alpha Bennet reads the message aloud for the other Alphas to hear.

'Alpha Bennet, Yiselda has agreed to take you and only you as a precaution into Pandora's Box tomorrow. Please cease any attack plans until you can see that the witches truly protect all of us, including you.

Nina, Luna of Shadow Crest,'

He scrunches the parchment up and smiles at Reaper, 'Tell her I look forward to it.'

Chapter 16

As she stands, Yiselda adds, 'I shall return tomorrow to lead Alpha Bennet to Pandora s Box,'

'We'll accompany you, Yiselda, and return to Shadow Crest later,' I say.

'Very well,' she says with a smile.

I need to see Alec, not just because I can't stop thinking about him, but also because I'm curious about this mark. I want to ask him why I keep thinking of him in a sensual light, but I can't acknowledge that I find him appealing. It just wouldn't be proper.

'May you should come with us this time?' I say.

'Yes!' May exclaims as she dashes over to join us.

'I'll be back soon,' I kiss Magnus,

'Don't keep me waiting too long,' he smiles.

'I won't,' I respond as I kiss him once more.

We port through the circle, following the witches and appear outside Pandora's Box. Upon entering,

May squeals in delight at the broom sweeping the floor.

'Does it ever stop sweeping?' I ask out of curiosity.

Yiselda laughs, 'No dear. It doesn't,'

'Hmm, very good,' I say, intrigued and enter the kitchen through the left door.

Yiselda, using her powers, makes everyone a hot cup of tea. The kettle, teaspoons and teacups float around the room toward the table.

'I'm going to go to the enchanted garden for a while,' I smile.

'Okay, give Star a pat for me,' Yiselda yells out as I leave the kitchen and walk down the hallway. I pass through the mirror, stop at the right door, and open it.

'Reaper, you stay here and keep a lookout. I'll be back, okay?'

'Where are you going?' He mind-links.

'I'll tell you later, I promise.' He flies off my shoulder and hops onto the ground.

'Just be quick, okay?'

I nod, 'Thanks, Reaper,' I smile.

'Materialise,' I say, imagining a book. I place it on the ground in the darkness in front of me. 'Sprouto Spawniate,' I say. The books multiply and grow in size and form a staircase. I flick my wand for light and close the door behind me as I walk up the stairs of books until I reach the large black door with the sigils drawn in place. I slowly open the door, careful not to smudge the markings.

The Grimghouls hiss, showing their teeth as I walk by. The dark silhouettes of the Shadow Reapers moan as if they are in agony. I can only just make them out.

'I knew you couldn't stay away from me long,' Alec says in his husky voice, sending a hot shiver down my spine.

'How did you know?' I say, stepping close enough to see his face with the dim light of my wand.

He smiles endearingly at me, 'That's a secret I'd like to keep for a while longer, but I'm delighted you're here. It's not often I get visitors. It's mostly Yiselda who visits each day to give me my daily nourishment. Sometimes but rarely, one of the other witches brings it to me, but they don't even acknowledge me,'

'Daily nourishment? You mean blood?' I say, a little anxious.

'You're a werewolf, so it's not like you don't go hunting and slaughtering rabbits and other rodents for your wolf-form nourishment,'
'That's very true,' I smirk.

A few moments pass, and I realise we have been gazing at each other silently. I blink and shake my head—the mark on my wrist warms up, spreading warm sparks through me.
I'm now as close as I can be to the bars and hold my wrist out towards Alec. 'You have done something to me. Please tell me what this mark is and what these strange feelings are. You have to tell me,' I demand.
He gently takes my arm, caresses his thumb over the mark and leans against the bars.
'This isn't just a mark, my love. This is my new destiny,' he says and places a kiss upon the mark. My body instantly feels on fire. The same way Magnus makes me feel. I pull my arm back and stare at him with a worried look.
'I don't understand,' I say.
'Once I am out of here, you will understand,' he says.
I just noticed I had subconsciously stepped close to the bars again, in reach of Alec. Our faces are inches apart.

'You don't seem to be afraid of me, Nina?' He whispers.

'Should I be?' I whisper back. It feels like a magnet is pulling us together, wanting us to be closer. I feel mesmerised staring into his light brown eyes. It feels like I have known him all my life.

His hand cups my left cheek.

'Yes, you should be,'

'Why?' I ask. Alec's head leans in closer, and his lips almost touch mine until Magnus comes to mind, and I jump back.

'Because you want me,' he says.

'No, I'm with Magnus. I love Magnus. I don't understand why I feel the same sensations around you that I feel with Magnus. Like we are destined mates?'

'That's because you are my destined love. Just like the Moon goddess, Selene chose you and Magnus to be together. She has also chosen us to be blood flames,'

'Blood flames?' I say, confused.

'When a werewolf finds their soulmates, their destined life partner. They are known as mates. It works the same way with vampires, except mates are called blood flames,' he gently explains.

'Are you saying that the moon goddess has made me a mate with Magnus and y-you?' I say, trembling.

'Technically, yes,' he says with a grimace. 'And just a note, I don't like sharing,' he says, pouting like a child.

'You're lying? How do you know this?' I'm in denial and refuse to believe this, any of this.

'You saw it, but you didn't realise it at the time. A vampire's eyes turn red and flicker when they glimpse their blood flame. You will see fire in our eyes. It puts you into a trance and makes you approach subconsciously. We'll stay that way until our vampiric mark is placed on your wrist. It signals to other vampires that you are blood-flamed or, in other words, taken. It's also where the term blood flames came from because of our flaming, blood eyes when we first see you,' He explains.

I touch Magnus's mark on my neck. It tingles. 'Just like a wolf marks your neck to let other wolves know you are taken,' he frowns. Then I touch the mark on my wrist, and it has the same tingly feeling. I gasp, and tears begin to glide down my cheeks. I shake my head and run towards the black door on the opposite side.

'Please, wait, my love, don't leave me just yet!' He pleads. His voice is sorrowful. I open the door, lock it behind me, and double-check that the sigils are still there. Reaper is waiting for me as I open the next door. As I close the door behind me, he leaps onto my shoulder.

He mind-links, 'You're crying?'

'I need to go to the enchanted garden,' I sob, open the middle door, and walk through the extensive spacious library until I find the double doors and enter the garden.

I sit in a grove of bushes, sobbing into my hands. Gnomes move closer every time I glance up to wipe my tears, yet they freeze like statues every time I gaze at them. I ignore them and cry until I feel a swarm of tiny hands on my legs and back. All of the gnomes appear to be frozen around me, yet they placed their hands on my legs and back to console me.

'Luna, you must tell me what has happened?' Reaper pleads.

I nod and hold my wrist, showing him the mark.

'You're a vampire's blood flame!' Reaper caws in shock and almost falls off my shoulder in horror.

Chapter 17

'Not just any vampire's blood flame, Reaper, the vampire king, Alec's blood flame,' I say.

'The vampire king, Alec! The first time you came here, I sensed something happened to you. Alec marked you, didn't he?'

I nod my head.

'I had no idea what he had done at the time.' He grasped my wrist and left a mark, and I couldn't stop thinking about him in the same way I couldn't stop thinking about Magnus. My body was drawn to him, and I desired to be near him. What am I supposed to do, Reaper? How will Magnus react when he learns that Alec is my second mate?'

'I wish I had the answer for you, Luna.'

May enters the enchanted garden along with the other witches.

'Wow! so beautiful. Look at that gnome!' May says and pokes its belly. The gnome doesn't move, but when no one is looking, his expression shifts to one of irritation. 'You weren't joking when you said there was a unicorn,' May says, approaching us. 'Nina, are you okay you look like you've been crying?' May adds.

'Oh, no, I think I'm just allergic to some of these flowers. My eyes went all red and puffy after I smelt them,' I force a laugh.

'Fern and the others are going to take me to see the Grimghouls, the Shadow Reapers and the vampire king next! Are you going to come with us?'

'You know, the vampire king isn't some kind of freakshow for you all to look at!' I lash out angrily. Everyone is staring at me strangely because of my outburst defending the vampire king. 'I apologise. I didn't intend to....'

'We understand you are under a lot of stress, Luna, with everything going on with the wolf council,' Fern empathises.

'I know, but I still should not have snapped like that. I'm sorry,' I grimace.

'It's fine. You don't have to go with us,' May says.

They leave the enchanted garden and enter the dungeon.

'Let's have a cup of tea,' I say to Reaper.

We walk into the kitchen and notice the iron kettle hovering above the fire. I grab a teacup, place it on the table, and fill it with one scoop of sugar and a teabag.

Waving my wand at the iron kettle, I exclaim, 'Lifto Levitatous.' It floats over to my teacup and fills it with hot water.

'You should probably tell Magnus about being the vampire king's blood flame,' Reaper says.

As I tremble at the thought, the teacup starts to wobble. I set the cup down and take a deep breath, attempting to relax.

'I can't tell him, Reaper, not just yet. There could be a way to break the bond?'

'I've never heard of a way to break the blood flame bond, but you could always reject Magnus and break the mate bond? That way, you would only have one lover instead of two?'

'Reaper!' I growl. 'I love Magnus, and I am his Luna. We grew up together and have known each other all our lives. My love for Magnus is not something I will throw away. Can't I reject Alec instead?'

'Doesn't work that way with vampires,' he says.

'Well, then how does it work?'

'All I know is that it's different with vampires,'

'That's not very helpful information, Reaper,' I sigh. 'Maybe we can find some information in the forbidden room back in Shadow Crest?'

'Perhaps,' he says.

Yiselda, May and the others return to the kitchen.

'I'm sorry if he frightened you, May. I don't know what's wrong with him. I've never seen him in that state before.' Yiselda says.

May is shaking. I stand up from my seat and run over to her.

'What happened? Are you okay?' I ask.

'I will be fine. It was a lot more terrifying than I thought it would be going into that dungeon,'

'How so?' I ask—my heart races with worry.

'The vampire king was distressed, pacing back and forth in his cell and pulling at his hair. He appeared to be quite anxious and was constantly muttering to himself.

As we approached, he turned savage, screeching loudly through the bars as if famished of blood, setting the Grimghouls off. They tried to attack us by advancing their arms through the bars and clawing ferociously at us. I didn't have a choice except to put the vampire king to sleep. And being the vampire king, he is stronger than most, so our sisters had to help cast the 'Dreamus Sleepous' spell as it had no effect on him even when I had cast it onto him myself.'

A dreaded feeling consumes me. I'm forcing myself not to run to Alec. What if they hurt him? Was it my fault he was distressed?

'Is he going to be, okay? Why would he be erratic like that?' I ask, clearly worried.

Yiselda laughs, 'My dear Luna, what has gotten into you? It's the vampire king, and you shouldn't worry yourself over him. But for what it's worth, he is not hurt. He is simply taking a nap and will hopefully return to his normal self once he awakes. He hasn't missed a meal, so I am confused about why he was in that state. Vampires do not die if they haven't consumed blood in a long time. They simply become erratic, losing all control of themselves,'

I force my tears back, 'I need to go home. Thank you for the tea, Yiselda,' I say and dash out the front door and enter the circle. May, Fern, Ria, Ela and Lilac appear behind me. But I don't wait for them. Instead, I race inside the packhouse and up to my room.

'Nina, is that you?' Magnus yells out.

'Um, yeah, it's me. I'm feeling exhausted. I'm going to go lie down for a while,' I say and climb under the covers and hug my knees.

The door creaks open, 'I know you've only been gone for a few hours, but I've missed you,' he says as he crawls beneath the blankets with me.

He pulls me in closer and nuzzles my neck as he snuggles up behind me. I turn to face him and caress his cheeks. I'm overcome with guilt and begin to cry.

'Nina, it will be okay. If you think Alpha Bennet and the wolf council will exile you from your own home and pack. Then he has another thing coming. I'd give up my Alpha status if it meant staying with you,' he says, wiping my tears away with his thumb.

'Magnus, I could never ask you to give Shadow Crest and your status away,' I sob.

'You wouldn't have to ask,' he says.

He kisses me passionately, and suddenly Alec's face flashes through my mind. I break the kiss and struggle for air.

'Nina, what is it?' Magnus says.

'I'm sorry, I need to go. I'll be back later,' I say, hurriedly putting my shoes back on. 'Skedaddle Dash,' I say before Magnus can respond.

I appear downstairs, and Reaper flies onto my shoulder.

'We need to go to the forbidden room and figure this out now,' I say to him and make a hasty descent to the basement. May and the others are concocting magical potions.

'Come to help make some love potion?' Lilac winks at me.

'No, sorry, not today. I have some things I need to do. I'll see you all later,' I say, stepping into the circle and teleporting into the forbidden room. I flick my wand for light. Reaper lands on the altar and keeps an eye on me while I leaf through dozens of books over the next two hours.

'There has to be information somewhere,' I say.

'Have you considered asking the vampire king himself?' Reaper suggests.

'Reaper, why didn't I think about that? Hey Alec, Vampire King, it's your blood flame here. I suppose you wouldn't tell me how to break the blood flame bond between you and me by any chance, would you?' I shake my head at Reaper. 'Could you imagine his reaction, Reaper? Sure, darling, let me do the honours for you and break it… I think it was quite obvious, Reaper, that he doesn't want to sever the bond and wants to be with me,'

'Okay then, how about this? They fight to the death. Whoever lives wins?'

'Reaper!' I growl

Chapter 18

I'm having trouble sleeping. I slip out of Magnus's embrace and sit on the balcony. I can't get my mind off seeing Alec tomorrow. I should be more concerned about Alpha Bennet and the witches' fate. My inner wolf is crying to be let out. Perhaps going for a run will help. Shifting, I try not to wake Reaper. I leap from the balcony and course my way through the woods of Shadow Crest.

My mind thinks of both Magnus and Alec. The notion of them both sends warm sparks through my body. Damn mate and blood flame bond! I can't get them out of my head.

I can see the lake ahead of me. At this hour of the night, it would be terribly cold. I rush up the slope at lightning speed and plunge into the lake. The ice-cold water overpowers me, but in a good way, as it cleanses my mind of the two men I want to be with.

The sun is slowly rising. I've been in the water for almost two hours. I'm semi-conscious and have become hypothermic. I don't want to get out of the water, though. I don't want to feel the guilt of thinking about Alec when I'm with Magnus. There is a howl in the distance. It's Magnus sending an alert out. I'm disoriented, and I'm wondering what the alert is for.

I'm barely afloat and feel myself slipping deeper into the lake. I know I have no option but to swim out of the lake at this point, but my paws refuse to move. My body completely submerges underwater, and I realise I'm drowning.

After a few moments, I feel the force of someone jumping into the water. I'm hauled out just as I'm going to drown.

Magnus yells, 'May, Josie, I found her!'

I manage to shift to my human shape, but I'm out of energy to move.

'Nina, please wake up!' He shakes me gently. For a brief period, my eyes open slightly, but I can't keep them open. I'm shivering uncontrollably.

'Magnus?' I murmur.

'Yes, Nina, it's me, and you're safe now,'

'You're so cold,' he says as he lifts me. He carries me to the packhouse while holding me tight to his chest.

Everyone rushes over to see us.
'Where was she? What happened to her?' Leon asks.
'I found her submerged in the lake. I think she has been in there for some time,'
'What would make her do something so careless, swimming at ridiculous hours in the lake in the dead of winter?' Leon asks.
'We will worry about why later. My priority is to get Nina warm.' Magnus says and enters the house. He places me on our bed, removes his clothes, and holds me in his arms. His body is like a heater on its own.
My body presses closer to his for more warmth. The shivering slowly dissipates. Magnus caresses my face until I fall asleep.

It's right after lunch when I wake. Magnus has not left my side. He gazes into my eyes. 'Nina, are you feeling better?' I nod. 'Can you tell me why you were in the lake?' he asks calmly. I start to tremble and shake my head no, holding back my tears. 'Nina, please, you have to tell me? Has something happened?' I don't want to lie to him, but I don't know how to tell him. I shake my head yes. 'Did someone hurt you?' He asks.

I can hear his heartbeat rapidly increase at the thought. I shake my head no. His body instantly relaxes. 'Okay, do you want to talk about it?' I shake my head no, giving him a solemn stare. 'The moment you are ready to tell me and talk about it, you will come straight to me, won't you?' I shake my head, yes, and he pulls me in for a tighter hug. 'I love you, Nina,'

'And I love you too,' I whisper.

We are interrupted by a knock.

'Zak, what exactly is it?' Magnus inquires.

'Alpha Bennet will be here soon,' he informs me.

'Okay, I'll be up and dressed in a moment then.'

Zak closes the door and returns downstairs.

As Magnus dresses, I sit up and reach for my clothes.

'What are you doing, Nina? You need to rest,'

'Yiselda and the others will need me at Pandora's Box just in case Alpha Bennet attempts anything,' I remind him.

He frowns, 'Surely, they can manage without you?'

'As a member of the Midnight Coven., I must be there and assist,'

'I'm just worried about you, Nina. You had hypothermia this morning and almost drowned,'

Stepping closer to Magnus, I wrap my arms around him. ''I'm sorry I scared you this morning. I didn't mean for that to happen,' I explain.

He kisses the top of my head. 'Just swear not to scare me like that again,'

'Promise,' I say quietly.

We walk downstairs together. Everyone approaches me.

'Are you all right, Luna?' Josie replies as she embraces me.

'I'm glad you are better now. Why were you in the lake last night?' May asks.

My mother and father approach me with sad expressions and embrace me. I speak up before they ask the same question as everyone else.

'Thank you, everyone, for all your concern. It means a lot to me. As for what happened, that's a conversation for another day.'

'But…' May says,

'That's final,' I say as loud thuds hammer on the door. As Magnus opens the door to see the wolf council, a blast of black mist flies over them, frightening them. Everyone ducks down as Reaper swoops over and lands on my shoulder.

'You need to control that thing of yours,' Alpha Bennet sneers, glaring at Reaper.

'This thing is a Shadow Raven and my familiar. His name is Reaper.' I retort.

Yiselda emerges behind them, 'Are you ready, Alpha Bennet?' She asks, scaring them even more.

We make an effort not to chuckle.

Alpha Bennet scoffs, 'Alpha Amir and Alpha Theaton will stay here with the rest of us. Let's go.' He says.

As we exit and follow Yiselda, Magnus escorts Alpha Amir and Alpha Theaton inside.

'To that circle over there,' Yiselda tells Alpha Bennet. He walks in front of her as they get closer. She pushes him into the circle while clutching his shirt, and they both vanish. We enter the portal and appear at Pandora's Box.

'Where on earth is this place?' Alpha Bennet asks.

'Fae Forrest,' Yiselda replies.

'Why have I never heard of Fae Forest before?'

'Because it's not on any map, it's a hidden location, and for a good reason. Only a few people know of this location.' She says.

We walk inside, and Alpha Bennet takes his time taking in all the items floating and moving around the rooms. He tilts his head at the self-sweeping broom.

'This way, if you don't mind, Alpha Bennet,' Yiselda says, hurrying him up.

We walk through the hallway, enter the large mirror, and watch as Yiselda opens the door on the right.

'There is nothing in there? It's just darkness. Is there even a floor to stand on in there?' Alpha Bennet asks.

Yiselda smiles at him and turns back to the dark empty room, 'Materialise,' she says. A book appears in her hand. She casts the next spell while Alpha Bennet gives her a weird look as he tries to figure out the use of the book.

'Sprouto Spawniate,' she says.

Alpha Bennet takes a step back in astonishment as he watches the staircase of books develop in front of his eyes. Everyone but me is smiling as we walk up the stairs.

Chapter 19

Part of me is excited and wants to see Alec, but the other part feels guilty and thinks of Magnus.

We come to a standstill in front of the dark wooden door.

'What do these symbols mean?' Alpha Bennet inquires.

'If the dark ones on the other side escape their cells, these markings will prevent them from exiting through this door,'

'Like an invisible forcefield?' He asks.

'Yes, it will also harm them, inflicting severe pain and injury if they try to force themselves through it.'

As Yiselda opens the door, he responds, 'I see.' Alec's sandalwood and sage scent waft out the door, past me. My body is telling me to run to him. I'm still exhausted from nearly drowning this morning. I muster my strength to keep my feet from running to him. My fists clench, and I walk behind everyone so they don't see me struggling to fight myself.

Grimghouls snarl at alpha Bennet and the others. I see I'm close enough for them to grasp me through the bars, yet they don't seem bothered by my presence. I'm curious as to why they wouldn't attack me.

'What are these vicious things? I've never seen them before,' Alpha Bennet says, taking a step back.

'Grimghouls, with their razor fangs and claws, they can rip someone to pieces in seconds,' Yiselda adds. Alpha Bennet trembles.

Alec's stare is scorching through me as we approach the Shadow Reapers. I smile at Lilac and keep my eyes down to avoid staring at him. Unlike the Grimghouls, the Shadow Reapers approach me. Yiselda gives me a strange look, and I shrug. They retreat to the rear of the cell as Reaper lets out a caw.

'I'm a Shadow Raven. They are drawn to me,' Reaper explains.

'Oh,' I say out loud, receiving more strange looks.

Yiselda explains to Alpha Bennet how they lurch down your throat and take over your mind and body, causing hallucinations.

'I can barely see them in the dark,' he says.

'Illumini,' Yiselda casts the spell of light, illuminating the cell. You can see the Shadow Reapers now. They are human silhouettes with black mist emanating from them in the same way as Reaper does. 'Dimulous,' she says, their cell now once again dark.

'I supposed it's time for you to meet their master, the vampire king,' Yiselda says, walking towards Alec's cell.

They approach the cell. I can see out my peripheral vision Alec's hands clenched around the bars, and his head is wedged between them. I remain behind everyone, keeping as much distance as I can. My hormones are raging as a result of his scent, and Alec appears he is also struggling to hold himself back. His hands tighten around the bars, and beads of sweat form across his forehead as he watches me.

'This is the vampire king?' Alpha Bennet sneers.

'Yes, it is him,' Yiselda confirms.

Alec suddenly focuses on Reaper on my shoulder and begins to laugh hysterically.

'Hello, Reaper. It's been a long time, my old friend,' he smiles.

Reaper caws.

'You know the vampire king?' I ask Reaper.

'Did I not mention that?' He mind-links.

'Um, no, you did not tell me that. Care to explain?'

Alpha Bennet scoffs, interrupting the mind-link between Reaper and me, 'He looks as weak as a wart on a toad's rear and only looks to be around twenty years old?'

Alec hisses and flashes his teeth at Alpha Bennet, causing him to back away. Alec then returns to staring at me intently.

'Appearances can be deceiving,' Yiselda says, 'He has been here for a long time, and his powers are phenomenal. It took the entire coven to get him in here using multiple spells at the same time,'

'How long has he been in here?' Alpha Bennet asks.

'Hundreds of years. I've lost count on how many years exactly.'

My heart sinks at the thought that Alec has been alone here for so many years. Finally, I look him in the eyes. As his eyes burrow into mine, my heart beats faster. It's as though we can peer into each other's souls. He has a sad and longing expression on his face. His eyes close, and he breathes in. I realise he is taking in my scent and is definitely feeling the same urges as me. It's evident to me he wants to hold me and touch me. I blush and look away before he opens his eyes.

'So, this vampire king here had let all these dark creatures on the loose to kill everyone hundreds of years ago?'

'According to the stories I've heard, he was once a magnificent King until he sought revenge after losing his blood flame Juniper to humans. She was a witch and was burned at the stake hours after Alec and Juniper met.'

I let out a gasp and stare solemnly at Alec. It's hurting him hearing the story. I can see it and sense it.

'Forth of vengeance, he summoned Shadow Reapers and Grimghouls and ordered vampires out to slay all humans.' Werewolves attempted to defend humans by preventing them from invading human territory.

Thousands of werewolves had perished, and the war was slipping away from them. Witches rushed in to aid, and we've been able to keep him here ever since. The vampires vanished and have been in hiding ever since. However, I have heard rare stories of people found dead with puncture marks on their necks. Vampires are still around. It's just that no one has ever lived after seeing them to tell the tale of their existence.

After a few centuries, werewolves had forgotten the vampire king, and he became little more than a terrifying fable, told to their pups each night. Werewolves eventually turned on us and almost wiped us all out.' Yiselda explains.

I've unknowingly moved closer to Alec's cell. My hand reaches towards his cheek. I have to touch him. Yiselda takes my wrist, looks at me strangely, and pulls me back towards her. Her grasp on my wrist is tight.

Alec hisses at Yiselda, but she ignores him.

'Now that you know he exists, you understand how important it is that we survive so that we may continue to keep Pandora's Box sealed from the rest of the world,'

'Why don't you just kill the king and those creatures?' Alpha Bennet asks.

'The vampire king cannot simply be killed. Even if we starve him, he doesn't die. Instead, he becomes erratic and loses his mind. Although they don't like sunlight, it also does not kill them,'

'What about a stake to the heart?' Alpha Bennet suggests.

'Well, if you want to go in the cell and risk your life trying to stake his heart, be my guest. But, even then, we don't even know if that will work,' Yiselda says. 'You'd probably be dead before you could blink since he has incredible strength and speed and would drain your blood in minutes,'

'What about all those creatures then?'

'They weren't always Grimghouls and Shadow Reapers. The Grimghouls are the Pixies of Silverfay Forest, where they and familiars reside. They are the only ones left to exist, and Shadow Reapers are souls from the dead that need to be returned to their resting place.

For many years, I've been researching spells in the hopes of reverting the pixies to their original forms and returning them to Silverfay Forest, as well as returning the souls of the shadow reapers to their resting places.

Hence, why witches before me chose to seal them all in this dungeon in hopes of restoring them back and keeping the vampire king under control, but now if you are satisfied, we shall return to Shadow Crest?'

Alpha Bennet's face contorts in thought as he stares at Alec, who won't take his gaze away from me. Alpha Bennet looks between us, perplexed as to why he is so interested in me.

'All right then, let's go back to Shadow Crest.' He agrees.

Chapter 20

Yiselda comes to a halt as we approach the circle to port back to Shadow Crest.

'Fern, Ela, Ria, Lilac, I would appreciate it if you could return to Shadow Crest with Alpha Bennet while I stay behind with Luna here,' she says.

'Sure, Yiselda,' they smile. Fern grabs Alpha Bennet by the back of his shirt and shoves him through the portal. I turn and giggle, looking at Yiselda, who is irritated and has her hands on her hips. My laughter stops.

'Uh oh,' Reaper mind-links.

'Is everything okay?' I ask her.

'What possessed you to approach the vampire king in such a manner? You seemed like you were about to touch him? Do you realise he has the ability to kill all of us, Luna, even you?' She claims.

'I'm sorry, I didn't intend to do that.' I couldn't help myself....'

'You couldn't help yourself,' she scoffs.

I glance to the ground with guilt and clutch my wrist, feeling the tingles. Perhaps if I show Yiselda, she'll be able to assist me in figuring out how to sever the bond? I'm immediately dizzy. I haven't recovered all of my strength after nearly drowning this morning. I stagger and grasp my head.

'Luna?' replies Yiselda, steadying me.

I concentrate and shake the dizziness away.

'I have something I need to show you,' I say, revealing my wrist to Yiselda and showing her the mark. She gives out the loudest shriek I've ever heard before falling back. She stands up, takes my arm, and pulls my wrist close to her face.

'It cannot be. Alec has marked you. You are the vampire king's blood flame,' staring at my wrist in disbelief, she finally looks at me. 'You have two mates!' she exclaims.

Taking my arm back, I walk away a few steps and solemnly stare up at the sky.

'Yiselda, I don't know what to do. It will destroy Magnus if he finds out I have a second mate, but I can't help these feelings towards Alec. I want to be with him too.' I explain.

She grabs my arm and yanks me back into the house.

'Where are we going?' I ask.

'You must sever your bond with Alec for your own good and protection. We need to ask Alec how to do that,' she adds as she pulls me up the staircase of books.

'Skedaddle Dash,' she says, making us blink from the dungeon's entrance and reappear on the other side outside Alec's cell.

Alec immediately emerges from the shadows of his cell and reaches his hand out for mine. 'Nina,' he says. I instinctively reach my hand out to take his, but Yiselda pulls me back.

'Alec,' she growls. 'Nina is Luna of Shadow Crest and fated mates with Magnus. You have to break the bond with Nina!'

'No,' he says firmly without hesitation.

'Alec, how do you suppose you will have a relationship with her behind these bars? If Magnus finds out, he won't allow her here again, and you know what will happen to Nina if she isn't near you frequently. For her sake, break the bond,'

Alec lunges at the bars scaring Yiselda back, 'I said no!' he yells.

'W-what will happen to me if we stay apart?' I ask.

Alec looks away with guilt.

'The blood flame draws you to your other half like the mate bond. You will begin to burn if you resist it or remain too far away from your blood flame for too long. It starts as a fever, but it steadily worsens until you eventually burn to death,'

I gasp and cover my mouth, 'Magnus would never cope without me. It would kill him,' I say.

'And it will kill me too if anything ever happened to you,' Alec says.

Alec and I stare solemnly at each other.

'If you don't break the bond. You know she will die, Alec,'

'No, she won't. Magnus will have to let us be together in order for her to live. Do you think he is willing to let her die if he loves her that much?' Alec retorts.

'Do you think Magnus is going to share his mate?' Yiselda argues.

'Our mate,' he corrects her.

I fall to my knees and cradle myself. Yiselda kneels beside me and rubs my back as I start to cry.

'If Alec doesn't break the mate bond, you will have to tell Magnus,' Yiselda says sympathetically.

Wiping my tears, I stand up to see Alec has retreated to the shadows of his cell. Approaching his cell, I grip the bars.

'Alec, please, breaking the bond is the only way for us to live and cease these feelings we both have for one other.'

Alec's hands reach through the bars with an instant flash, cupping my face, his lips crashing onto mine.

A euphoric feeling flows through my body and his, and my inner soul melts from his kiss.

I've always felt happy with Magnus, and I know I'm in love with him, but something was always missing in my heart, and now, kissing the vampire king, I realise that the missing piece of my soul was my second mate, Alec.

I'm overcome by the overpowering sensation of being whole with Alec and Magnus. We break the kiss for breath, and I take a step back, swaying and collapsing. Reaper settles alongside me on the ground.

'Luna!' Yiselda and Alec exclaim simultaneously. Yiselda cradles my head in her lap.

'Luna,' Yiselda says again as she tries to wake me.

'Yiselda, let me out, let me help her!' Alec begs.

'Alec, you will never be free from that cell, and I certainly won't let you anywhere near the Luna,'

Alec scowls at her, 'I will make sure you will regret keeping me from my treasured blood flame, Yiselda,' he angrily says.

Yiselda ignores him and waves her wand over me, 'Awaken,' she says. Alec watches closely as my eyes flicker awake. Yiselda helps to sit me up.

'Where am I?' I say, taking a glance around. Then the memory of kissing Alec flashes through my mind. I raise my eyes to Alec, who has a troubled expression on his face.

'Are you okay, Nina? Yiselda refused to let me out to help you,' he says.

'I haven't been the best since this morning. I'm sorry, Magnus insisted I stay home and rest, but I didn't listen to him,'

'What happened this morning?' Yiselda asks.

'I-I almost drowned in the lake… before sunrise,'

'You almost died?' Alec asks.

'Isn't it currently the middle of winter in Shadow Crest?' Yiselda asks.

I nod my head, 'I couldn't sleep, and I couldn't stop thinking about Alec and felt so guilty. I wanted the longing for Alec to stop, so I shifted and went for a run and stayed in the icy cold water of the lake for as long as I could. It helped keep my mind off Alec. Unfortunately, I was in there too long, and when I tried to swim out of the lake, I couldn't move my paws. I was too cold. Soon after, I began to sink underwater, and Magnus found me as I blacked out. He took me home and kept me warm in bed until not long before the meeting with Alpha Bennet. He wanted me to stay and rest, but I refused,'

'How come he didn't tell me? I would have made you remain at home as well,' Yiselda says.

'I imagine he didn't have time to tell you,'

Yiselda looks at Alec, 'This is more reason for you to break the bond, Alec. Her life has already been put at risk once, and putting it off will only further risk her life. End it now, or I'll be sure to punish you,' she warns.

Alec glares at Yiselda, 'No,' he repeats.

'Luna, this leaves you with no choice. We have to inform Magnus of your second mate.' she says.

Chapter 21

'Nina, wait before you go. You will come back to see me tomorrow?' Alec pleads.

I approach the bars and grasp his hand in mine, 'I'll come back as soon as possible.'

Yiselda, Reaper and I leave Pandora's Box and port to Shadow Crest.

The wolf council are still talking to Magnus in the dining room. I take my seat next to Magnus. He takes my hand, kisses it, and resumes his focus on Alpha Bennet.

'Yiselda, I informed Alpha Amir and Alpha Theaton about what I witnessed in Pandora's Box, confirming its contents. So, we've agreed that witches can live in Shadow Crest for the time being,'

'For the time being?' Yiselda is confused.

'Yes, for now,' he answers as he stands up. 'We'll say our goodbyes and stay in touch,' he says as he walks towards the packhouse's entrance. Alpha Amir and Alpha Theaton are right behind him as he walks out the door.

Ela, Fern, Ria, and Lilac rejoice and hug each other as they learn they will be able to stay in Shadow Crest.

'With that, I'll be downstairs concocting some potions!' Ria says, 'I'll help,' says Lilac. 'Me as well!' Ella and Fern say. 'Don't forget about me,' May says as she dashes downstairs after them.

'Well, that's good news for the girls,' Yiselda says, smiling.

Reaper flies from my shoulder and lands on the window ledge as Magnus pulls me in for a hug and gives me a strange look, 'You smell different, like sandalwood and something else I can't put my finger on,'

I give Yiselda a worrisome look. She nods, indicating to tell him.

'Magnus, there's something I need to tell you,' I say.

'Sure, what do you want to tell me?' He smiles.

I look into his mesmerising green eyes. My hands start to tremble, and my eyes water. Magnus can see something isn't right.

'What is it, Nina?'

'Can we go somewhere private? And with Yiselda as well,' I add.

He looks to Yiselda. She nods.

'Sure, let's go to our office,' he gently takes my hand. Sparks tingle up my arm.

Entering the office, he takes his seat, and I take mine next to him. Yiselda sits on the two-seater couch against the wall.

There is an awkward silence while Magnus looks between Yiselda and me.

'So, which one of you are going to tell me what's going on?' he says, breaking the silence.

Yiselda and I exchange glances, and she nods again for me to speak.

'Do you recall how you noticed this symbol on my wrist and when I told you it appeared when Alec held my wrist?'

'Yes, you said it slightly burned at first, and you felt a little strange?' He says.

'Well, um,' I say, holding back a sob. I take a deep breath. 'Alec marked me. I'm his blood flame,' I say with a trembled voice.

Magnus gives me an odd look and grabs my wrist, saying, 'I don't get it? What is a blood flame, and why would he inflict this mark on you?'

'You know how werewolves mark their soulmates?' I say. He nods, 'Well, for vampires, they mark their blood flames.'

There is complete silence as Yiselda and I watch Magnus process it all. You can tell from his face he is trying to understand what I am saying. Suddenly he stiffens, and his face pales.

'No… no, no, no, no,' he says abruptly, standing up, his hands tugging at his hair. 'How? You can't?' He struggles to speak and continues to panic. Then he comes to a standstill and anxiously glances down at me, fumbling with my fingers.

'You had said you felt strange that day. In what way did you feel strange?' He asks with a hurt look in his eyes. I can see he already knows the answer but is hoping I tell him otherwise.

'B-because since that day, I feel the mate bond with Alec. I feel a magical sense of overwhelming wholeness as if I could never live without either one of you. My heart and body tell me I'm meant to have both of you. The bond has been pulling me and urging me to go to him as it does with you.' I explain.

Magnus casts a glance out the window. I can hear his laboured breathing. His hands are gripped so tightly that I can see blood dripping.

'He's not going to be able to have you, Nina. You are MINE!' he shouts as he approaches me. He grabs my shoulders with his bleeding hands and pulls me into his chest.

'We'll fix it, Nina. You'll never have to see him again.'

Before I can tell him it won't be possible since it will kill me, he smells the sandalwood scent on me and takes a step back, a scared expression on his face.

'That scent, it's his, isn't it?'

I nod but avoid making eye contact. Magnus, on the other hand, slowly lifts my chin to look at him.

'Nina, please tell me nothing has already happened between you two? Please give me another explanation as to why his scent is all over you!?'

Tears stream down my face onto his fingers as he holds my chin, 'I-I can't give you another explanation.' I cry.

The hurt that appears in Magnus's eyes is unbearable to watch. I try to look away. But now I see pain and anger in his eyes.

'I'm sorry, Magnus, Alec kissed me, and I struggled against the bond to stop the kiss from continuing,' I confess.

'Did you like it?' He frowns.

'W-what?'

'You heard me, Nina. Did you enjoy the kiss?' He yells.

I fall to my knees crying and look up at my beloved Magnus, 'It felt euphoric, the same as kissing you.'

Magnus storms out of the packhouse.

'Magnus, please!' I chase after him, but Yiselda grabs me.

'Luna, he needs to process everything. It will help if you give him some time alone,' she suggests.

I hesitantly nod. I want to hold Magnus and tell him I love him no matter what. My inner wolf whimpers, wanting to comfort his wolf.

Magnus didn't come back to our room that night. I spent most of the night peering out the window, wondering where he was and when he'd return.

'Reaper, please try and find him for me?' I say to him in the moon tree. I watch as Reaper flies into the night in search of Magnus.

Will Magnus ever forgive me? What if he wants to leave me? Is he going to reject me and find a new mate? All these thoughts and more flow through my mind until I fall asleep from fatigue.

I look onto Magnus's side of the bed as I wake. He isn't there. Reaper is on my window sill.

'I couldn't find him, Luna.' Reaper mind-links.

I run downstairs to see if he is having breakfast. Everyone else is eating breakfast, but Magnus is nowhere to be found.

'Good morning, Luna,' everyone says.

'Has anyone seen Magnus?' I ask with a slight tremble in my voice that everyone picks up.

'Isn't he in bed?' Josie asks.

'Um, no, I thought he might be down here eating breakfast,' I say.

'Is everything okay?' Flint asks.

I'm not sure if I should inform them Magnus is upset because I'm now also mates with the vampire king. I solemnly nod and force a small smile. 'He's probably out having a run in wolf form.'

Everyone nods and eats their breakfast. My appetite had disappeared. All I could think about was wanting to know if Magnus was okay, but I already know he isn't.

I'd be upset too if he came home and told me he had a second mate. How am I ever going to make us okay again? I burst into tears and run up the stairs, shocking everyone at the table. I enter my room and close the door behind me.

Chapter 22

I'm sitting against the door when I hear a gentle knock.

'Luna, it's May, Josie and the witches here. We have come to see if you are alright. It's not like you to burst into tears and run away like that,'

'Magnus is the one you should all be worried about,' I sob.

'Why is that, Luna? Has something happened to him?' May asks, concerned.

'I've done something terrible. Magnus will never forgive me,'

'I'm sure there is nothing in this world he wouldn't forgive you for,' May reassures me.

'Does that include cheating on him?' I say.

They all gasp and whisper to one another.

'Luna, I think you need to let us in and tell us what has happened so we can help you,'

'I'm a horrible person May. Why would you want to help me?'

'Because you are my sister, and you are not a horrible person. You are the sweetest, kindest, most understanding person I have ever met,' she retorts.

'That's right,' Everyone agrees.

Slowly, I stand and unlock the door. The girls all wrap their arms around me for a hug.

We all climb onto my massive bed, plump the cushion and get ourselves comfortable as they ready themselves to hear what I am about to tell them.

May wipes the tears from my face.

'The day I first went to Pandora's Box, something happened to me while we were in the dungeon. Do you remember when Alec held my wrist?'

'Yeah, you were insane being that close to him in the first place,' Ria chuckles but pauses when she notices my serious expression.

'He had marked me,' I say, holding my wrist for them all to see. They all furrow their brows, gazing closer to my wrist and shoving each other out of the way. Lilac tumbles off the bed onto the floor.

'I'm okay,' she adds as she crawls back onto the bed.

'So, what exactly does that mark mean?' May asks.

'It means Alec the vampire king is my blood flame. Alec is my second mate,'

'What!?' They all say. Everyone but May falls off the bed in shock.

Once they regather on the bed, they all look at each other and back at me.

'I feel the mate bond with Alec the same way I feel it with Magnus. My mind and body are yearning to be with both of them. Alec refuses to break the bond between us, and I don't know how to break it. Then we kissed, and it was so magical and amazing like I was kissing Magnus. I told Magnus about Alec being my second mate. He was angry and upset, which of course he would be, but I haven't seen him since.'

May wraps her arms around me, 'It will be okay. We will help you figure this out, won't we, girls?' They all nod and give me sympathising looks. 'We should tell Dad so that the warriors can find him?' She suggests.

'What will Mum and Dad think of me having two mates, May? They will be so ashamed of me,'

'No, they won't be. None of this is your fault, and there is a reason you have been given two mates, Nina. The moon goddess has willed it,' she says, making me feel less guilty.

'I can't believe the vampire king is your mate,' Lilac says. 'I get he is handsome and all, but he is a vicious murderer, Luna. He is evil,'

'He has been nothing but kind and gentle towards me, Lilac, and even so, he has spent hundreds of years alone in that dungeon and lost his first blood flame, who was killed at the hands of humans. If someone purposely killed Magnus, I would probably do everything in my power to kill whoever was responsible too,'

Lilac doesn't know what to say.

'I think Lilac just wants you to be very careful around Alec, that's all,' Ria says.

'My main focus is to find Magnus and have him home with me where he belongs.' I say.

Everyone nods in agreement.

'Then what are we all doing in here then? We will split up and all search for him,' Fern says.

Josie dashes downstairs while the rest of us 'Skedaddle Dash' and appear out the front. Josie frowns with her hands on her hips. 'That's not fair,' Josie pouts.

'Life is never fair, Josie,' May says.

Josie and I shift into our wolves. I'll be able to pick his scent up better this way. The witches all squeal and start patting Josie and me. Next thing you know, we are on our backs, suckered in with belly rubs until May clears her throat at the witches.

'Oh, yeah, Magnus, right,' Ela says.

Fern's cat jumps onto her shoulder, and they run into the distance. Everyone has dispersed, going separate ways.

I sprint to the summit of the mountain. He may be staying at one of the camping lodges. I dash in and out of the woods, hoping to get a whiff of his scent, but to no avail. I search every site and shelter and find no trace of him.

I sit and mope, trying to think of where he could be and where I would go if I were upset. Then it hits me Shadow Crest Lake, where we have shared so many fond memories. I dash down the hill through the woods until I reach the lake. I pick his scent up straight away and race towards him, sitting on the lake's edge.

My wolf whimpers, and I lower myself resting my head on his lap. He looks down at me, and I see he hasn't slept. Bags have formed under his eyes; his hair is all scruffy, and his eyes are puffy from all the tears. I whimper again, telling him I'm sorry.

He lifts me into his chest as he holds me close. I shift back into human form and place my hand on his cheek. Sparks fly between us. He pushes his face further against my hand taking in the blissful feeling.

'Although I feel so hurt and broken right now, I know none of this is your fault, Nina. We will work through this together.' We kiss passionately and make love.

Returning to the packhouse, we take our time. Before we enter, I come to a halt. 'I want you to know that Josie, May and the witches all know. I told them this morning,' I say.

'Good, because the more of us who know, the more of us who can assist us find out how to sever the tie between you two,' he continues.

We enter the home to find the others discussing where they had looked and searched. 'You found him, Luna,' Lilac beams.

'Thank you all for your concern. As you know, it's a lot to take in, and it took some time to absorb it all,' Magnus says.

'Of course, Alpha,' Lilac says.

Magnus turns to me, 'Let's have some lunch, then we can talk privately and see what resolutions we can come up with,' he says.

Once our lunch is finished, we enter our office and close the door. Magnus sits on the two-seater couch. I sit next to him, and he pulls me onto his lap.

Part of me is currently yearning for Alec, while the other part of me is happy and content being this close to Magnus.

'I don't want you going back to Pandora's Box,' he says calmly.

'But!' I say. Magnus presses his finger against my lips.

'Until we figure out how to sever the bond, I can't have you going there. I can't have you near him,'

'Magnus, I think it would be better if Yiselda could join this conversation to give you more insight. It's not going to be as simple as just not going near him, and what if it takes months or even years to figure out how to break the bond?'

'Then that's how long it will be until you return to Pandora's Box,'

'Magnus, Pandora's Box is my second home now. There will be times I may have to be there to help Yiselda and the others,'

'Then they will have to do it without you,'

'Magnus, please, let's talk to Yiselda and see what she has to say,'

'Yiselda isn't my mate, nor does she have any authority over me, Nina. You are not returning to Pandora's Box, and that is final.' He growls.

Chapter 23

I throw myself from his lap, dash to our bedroom, slam the door behind me, and sit on the balcony. Reaper takes flight from his moon tree and lands on the railing.

'I'm guessing things aren't going so well?'
He mind-links.

'No, he won't let me go back to Pandora's Box until the bond between Alec and me is severed.'

'What if it's unbreakable?' Reaper says.

'Then I'll have no option but to go against Magnus's wishes and meet Alec, or I can wait it out and eventually die from being separated from Alec for too long,'

I spend the following days primarily in the basement concocting potions practicing spells, and reading Mysteria: The history of supernaturals to avoid Magnus. My mind and body are constantly fighting me to rush to

Magnus and be with him, but they are also fighting me to go to Pandora's Box and be with Alec. I already feel like I've betrayed Magnus from the kiss Alec and I shared. I don't want to betray him again and defy him to see Alec in Pandora's Box. Every day it becomes worse, but I push past it and concentrate on making potions in the bubbling cauldron.

Ela, Fern, Lilac and Ria have come down many times over the few days to help me, but I sent them away every time, telling them I needed to be by myself. Another two days pass. Magnus has been trying to talk to me at every opportunity. 'I'm not ready to talk about it, Magnus,' I say each time. I let him still hug me and kiss me because I love him, and it brings some comfort to me. Returning to the basement, my body begins to heat up, but I ignore it thinking it's from all the steam and plumes of smoke and continue my work. Reaper has been sitting on his perch I made him. He is the only one I have allowed to stay by my side.

'You should get some rest, Luna. You've been working on this for more than five days. You don't appear to be in good health,' He mind-links.

I ignore him, but he continues to speak. 'Perhaps you could shift and go for a run, and I'll fly beside you?' he says.

Sweat beads collect on my face and torso. 'It's boiling down here,' I complain.

'How about we walk outside for some fresh air?' He says. I cave and nod. I manage to mutter 'Skedad' before slumping to the floor. I've suddenly become exceedingly weak and unable to cast a spell.

'Luna! I'll get help,' Reapers says.

'No, don't do that. All I want is Magnus and Alec,' I whimper.

'I can get Magnus for you.' He adds as he rushes up the stairs, leaving little time for me to say no.

Reaper caws furiously as feet stampede below. Magnus gets down on his knees at my side and places his hand on my arm. 'How come she's so hot? Is she sick?' Magnus asks Reaper, then realises he and Reaper cannot mind-link.

Magnus picks me up and carries me up the stairs while yelling for help. May and Lilac come running over to us. 'Magnus, what's the matter with Luna?' Lilac asks.

'I'm not sure. Reaper came up to me wildly cawing. I followed him down the basement and discovered her on the floor. She is unbearably hot to the touch. I'm struggling to hold her any longer. She is burning my skin,' he says.

'Take her to her room and place her in a cold bath. I'll go to Pandora's Box and bring Yiselda back with me,' May says.

Magnus can't remove my clothes as the sweat and heat make them stick to my skin. He turns the water on and places me in the bath, and holds my head up with one hand. He uses his other hand to trickle cold water onto my face.

Magnus lifts me out of the ice-cold bath and puts a towel over me. He rests his palm against my temple. 'You're still flaming hot, Nina,' he exclaims, horrified.

A knock comes from our bedroom door. 'It's May, and I'm here with Yiselda,' she adds.

'Please send her in quickly,' Magnus begs, his voice shaking with fear.

Yiselda enters the bathroom and stares at Magnus, soaking wet on the floor with me on his lap.

She speaks with a heavy sigh, 'It's begun,' she says.

'What has begun?' Magnus asks.

'Did Luna not warn you that the blood flame will continue to pull her and urge her to Alec and that if she resists it for too long or fights it, there will be implications?'

'I knew she'd be battling their bond, but she never mentioned any negative effects?'

'When you resist it or stay away from your blood flame for too long, you physically start to burn. It begins as a fever, then your body continues to heat up, and you die,'

'She's going to die!' Magnus snarls. 'Argh,' he groans as he places me on the tiled floor. He glances down at his scorched hands from holding me.

'What do we do? How can I help her?' He pleads.

'The only way to prevent her death is to bring them together,'

'What! There has to be another way,' he says.

'The only other option is to break the bond, but we don't know how to, and it appears that we don't have much time left. If you wish to save Luna, you must bring her to Pandora's Box right now,' she warns.

Magnus growls and battles his inner demons. He doesn't want me near Alec, but he also doesn't want me to die. With no choice, he grabs a blanket and lifts me with it to avoid his hands being burnt from skin contact. Yiselda dashes out the front door. Reaper and Magnus rush after her. Yiselda grabs the back of Magnus's shirt and pulls him into the circle as they approach.

For a brief period, my eyelids flutter open, and I glimpse someone else walking out of the portal, but they don't follow us inside. Instead, whoever it was darted into nearby shrubs.

I extended my arm and gestured to the bushes, hoping to draw the attention of whatever was lurking there. But, with no time to spend, Magnus ignores his surroundings and my arm's motion and rushes into the door.

He is captivated by the enormous mirror Yiselda stepped through, but he does not have time to linger and enjoy it before leaping through.

Yiselda opens the door on the right and says, 'Materialise,' and a book emerges, 'Sprouto Spawniate,' she adds, dropping the book at her feet. Magnus steps back as the book grows into a staircase. Reaper flies ahead and hovers by the dark wooden door.

'I must warn you, Magnus, Alec is in a worse state. You mustn't be afraid to hand her over to him. Blood flames will never hurt each other, no matter what,'

'What do you mean he is in a worse state?'

'I have been trying to persuade him to sever the bond or at least tell me how to do it. But, because he refuses, I've been depriving him of his daily nourishment of blood, which leads vampires to become erratic and savage,' she says and opens a large black door.

'I don't think I like the sound of any of this, Yiselda,' he says, following her through the dungeon. He sees the Grimghouls as he walks past. 'They are more vicious-looking than I ever imagined them to be,' he says.

'Don't get too close to them. If not your whole arm, they will rip your hand off, given the opportunity.'

We can hear agonising moans emanating from further up as we approach the Shadow Reapers, who are spell-sealed in their area of the dungeon.

'Alec,' I murmur.

Magnus stiffens, and a sombre expression develops on his face as he approaches the cell where Alec is.

Alec snarls and hisses. He appears to be physically and emotionally warring with himself. Yiselda was correct when she defined his current situation as erratic and savage.

Chapter 24

'This is supposed to be the vampire king? Yiselda. I'm not handing Nina over to that monster,'

Alec pauses, stares at Magnus, and snarls his fangs. Magnus expands his wolf teeth, and he growls in response.

'Now is not the time for a snarl off,' Yiselda says to Alec and Magnus. Alec drops his eyes to Nina lying weak in the arms of Magnus. His expression softens, and he reaches out to touch Nina, but Magnus steps aside and pulls me closer to his chest. 'It burns,' I gasp, biting my lip. It bleeds. My skin feels as though it is on fire. I open my eyes and tilt my head to see Alec looking at me longingly. His skin is red and covered with blisters, and I can see blisters forming on my arms. As I weep, the pain becomes unbearable.

'It's okay, Nina,' Magnus replies as he prepares to remove the blanket he's using to hold me.

'Alec, you must stand aside so we can place her in the cell with you,' Yiselda commands. Alec moves to the cell's rear, where he can't be seen.

'There is a spell in place at the entrance of his cell. Do you see the line of salt here?' Yiselda asks Magnus.

Magnus nods.

'Do not break the line. Place Nina over it and then step back immediately.'

Yiselda unlocks the door, and it creaks as she pulls it open. Magnus hesitantly stands at the entrance, his hands tremble as he is about to give me to the person he loathes, the very one he doesn't want me near, my second mate.

Removing the blanket, he ignores the burn that heats his flesh and gently lays me on the other side of the line. A tear falls from his eye and lands on my cheek. My hand touches his cheek. 'I love you, Magnus,' I say.

'I love you too, Nina,' he says and steps back.

Yiselda closes the cell door and locks it just as Alec swoops in like a flash of light and snatches

Nina up, returning to the shadows of his cell swiftly. The moment Alec swooped me up, the burning pain immediately subsided and was replaced with sweet, warm tingles. Alec cradles me in the corner. His back turned to the cell bars.

As he caresses my face, I can see his skin is healing. I cup my hand over Alec's, and he pulls me closer to him.

We gaze into each other's eyes. His aren't his usual light brown but primarily black. I can see he is straining himself from doing something, but I'm not sure of what.

Our lips draw closer to one another, the blood from my lip drips down my chin, and his eyes momentarily light up. And I realise he wants blood, my blood, and is fighting himself from taking it.

I smash my lips onto his and kiss him fiercely as he savours every drop of blood from my lips. He tenderly grips and sucks onto my bottom, bleeding lip with his as we eventually separate, not wanting it to finish.

As I instinctively submit to Alec, my head tilts up. On my unmarked side, his teeth skim across my nape. The tingling sensation that floods through my body cause me to gasp. His teeth suddenly sink in, and he moans from the sensation of drinking my blood. He withdraws his teeth and looks endearingly into my eyes. Raising my hand to his face, I gently wipe the blood drips from Alec's lips.

'My, Nina, my darling, my Queen,' he says.

Reaper caws and looks pleased that Alec has become my second mate.

'Alec,' I say and wrap my arms around him. We spend some time in a loving embrace before Alec licks the puncture marks he made on my neck. My body arches and I gasp at the thrilling feeling that soars through my body.

Magnus had walked over to the Shadow Reapers before we had kissed as he couldn't bear to watch us. Usually, a mate would feel horrendous pain when the other mate became intimate with another person. He thought it was odd he felt no physical pain, just jealousy.

We kiss passionately again, and when we part, I notice my skin has completely healed along with Alec's. Magnus storms over to the bars.

'That's enough, now give me back, my mate,' he scowls.

'Magnus,' I say, standing up. Alec grabs me and holds me to his chest.

'She is my blood flame,' Alec says firmly.

They glare at one another. 'Alec, it's okay. Magnus is my mate, and I need to go back to him,'

Alec cups my face with his hands, 'When will you be back?' he asks.

'Tomorrow,' I say. Alec looks at Magnus for confirmation. He squeezes the bars.

'Nina is my soul mate. She is my whole world. If bringing her back here each day keeps her alive, then so be it,' he growls, clearly not pleased with the concept but also knowing he has no other choice for the time being.

As I approach the cell door, Alec immediately spins me around and kisses me gently one final time before I see him again. Magnus is emitting a deep growl. Yiselda unlocks the door, and I gently walk over the line to leave the cell. Magnus quickly throws his arms around me and kisses my forehead and the opposite side of my neck, nuzzling into my nape. Alec is the one who lets out a deep growl this time.

'I'm sorry,' I say to Magnus as I look at him.

'It's not your fault. It had to be done,' Magnus replies softly, attempting to mask his pain.

'Let's go home and spend some time together. Just you and me,' I say.

He nods and grabs my hand in his as he leads me out of the dungeon. We enter the portal and spend the afternoon swimming at Shadow Crest Lake and climbing the most prominent trees we can locate, just as we did as kids.

We don't spend a single moment apart till we return to Pandora's Box the next day.

Knowing how to access the dungeon, I don't wait for Yiselda.

'I'll wait here at the entrance,' Magnus frowns, not wanting to see me near Alec.

I cup his face and kiss his lips. 'I'll be back soon,' I say.

I take the key hanging on the far wall, unlock the cell, and step over the salt line. Before I see Alec, he has already swept me off my feet and smothering my face in kisses.

'Alec,' I giggle.

'I've missed you,' he says.

'I missed you too,' I say.

We kiss, and he strokes my face with his thumb. 'I wish I could take you somewhere wonderful, like for a picnic on a mountain top or a dance beneath the stars,' he says thoughtfully.

'I wish I could just get you out of this dungeon,' I sigh. 'Did you really set those creatures onto the humans all those years ago?' I ask.

Alec looks away for a moment, then nods his head with regret.

'Can you tell me what happened? Can you tell me about Juniper?' I ask.

'It might be easier if I show you instead,' he says.

I'm confused until he shuts his eyes and hovers his hands slightly over each side of my head. Then, a ball of light appears and blinds me. When I open my eyes, I'm no longer in the dungeon but travelling along a cobblestone path in a village. There are individuals on horses everywhere and ladies on foot, holding shoals over their heads and baskets packed with bread and fruit.

A beautiful young woman runs into me, shouts, 'Sorry,' and keeps running. I chase after her as she rushes up the road and into a little cottage dwelling. 'Sorry, I'm late, grandma,' she apologises.

'Juniper, will you ever be on time?' her grandmother says.

Juniper laughs, 'Probably not, Grandma,' she says. I raise my head over the window sill to peer through it.

Juniper stuffs a loaf of bread and a couple of small bottles into the basket. They look just like potions.

'You need to hurry along Juniper, and get these healing potions to the Hillsbury home. If you go now, you will be home before dark. I don't want those creatures of the night capturing you,'

'Creatures of the night, really Gran. I think you've had too much rum,' Juniper smiles.

'Perhaps, Juniper, but I heard more people were found dead this morning with those markings on their necks. You can never be too cautious,' she advises.

'I'll be cautious, grandma, and I'll leave immediately to be home before nightfall,' Juniper replies, kissing her grandmother on the forehead.

'Juniper, remember, we may be witches, yet even humans can burn us at the stake. So, who knows what these creatures of the night are capable of doing to us.' she says.

I feel the same trepidation as Juniper does at her grandmother's words.

Chapter 25

Juniper departs from the cottage and strolls for an hour through the forest, eventually arriving in a valley with another settlement. I covertly follow behind her. She knocks on the door of a wood lodge.

'Juniper,' A respectable gentleman greets her and welcomes her inside the house. Another resident of the house is hacking and gasping for air.

'I was terrified I wouldn't receive the potion on time. Florence is on the verge of death,' Mr Hillsbury claims.

I pop my head up and observe Juniper and the gentlemen enter a room with an elderly lady in bed via a window. She is quite pale, coughing, and gasping for breath. Juniper arranges the basket on the bed and takes a healing potion. She extracts the cork from the bottle and proceeds to elevate the lady's head.

'Drink this, Florence. It will cure you of your illness,' Juniper asserts.

Florence initially struggles but eventually consumes the potion. Within minutes, her cheeks have taken on colour, and her eyes have become bluer. She rises to her feet and crosses her arms across her chest.

'I can breathe normally once again, and my chest feels clear,' she beams.

'Florence, it worked,' the gentleman adds, clasping Juniper's hands in his. 'I'd want to express my gratitude to you, Juniper, and your grandmother,' he continues.

'You're very welcome, Mr Hillsbury,' Juniper smiles.

Florence rises from the bed and joins her husband in walking Juniper out.

'It's already becoming dark,' Juniper observes as the sky darkens.

'Mr Hillsbury,' his neighbour says as he limps up the path.

'It's lovely to see you, George,' Mr Hillsbury says with a smile and a nod of his hat.

'Florence, your wife. She is out of bed walking? The doctor said she was so sickly she would die by tis very night. I don't understand,' George says. 'I came to offer my condolences to you, but here she stands fitter than a fiddle,'

'It's a miracle, isn't it?' Florence says. 'Juniper gave me medicine that cured me straight away,' she says without thinking of the consequences of her words. Her husband attempts to elbow her to stop her from talking.

'No medicine would do such a thing,' George says, glaring at Juniper.

Juniper trembles and takes a step back.

'Dear, I believe it is a bit implausible to claim you were suddenly cured.' Mr Hillsbury responds uncomfortably, 'Juniper was here all day attempting to mend you.' Florence casts a puzzled glance at her husband.

'I must be going now. Grandma wants me home before dark, and as you can see, the moon is rising,' I say, turning and stepping onto the path. George snatches her arm, causing her to fall over and drop the basket. The bread and a bottle of healing potion roll out. George picks up the bottle and inspects it reading the label and pulling the cork off. He sniffs, then drinks it.

Juniper's and Mr Hillsbury's faces are flushed with fear. As George approaches her, Juniper rises to her feet, his limp leg now healed. George comes to a halt and stares down at his leg before returning his gaze to Juniper.

'Impossible, my limp has gone,' He looks at the bottle in his hand, then at Juniper. 'This isn't medicine. This is a magic potion. You're a witch!' He points his finger at Juniper.

Juniper runs frightened from the village as George creates a commotion causing neighbours to come out of their houses. Men follow George, chasing after Juniper. She runs as fast as she can and knows they will go straight to her house to search for her. She knows they will burn her at the stake.

'I'm sorry, grandma, I can't go home,' she whispers into the wind. A shimmering breeze swirls around the fog of her breath like a spell, collecting her words and delivering her message to her grandmother.

Juniper abandons the trail and flees into the woods, eluding the horde of men.

She falls to her knees, becoming fatigued to walk any further. There are odd and unsettling noises all around her. She notices two crimson eyes looking at her from the darkness when she glances up. The eyes flash like a flame, and I immediately recognise them as Alec's.

Alec swoops forwards and covers Juniper's mouth with his palm as she screams.

'My blood flame, I've been looking for you for many years,' he says.

Juniper trembled in his arms. He carefully takes his hand away from her mouth. She gives him an odd expression as she touches her mouth, which tingles from his contact.

'Why do I have this sensation?' she sniffles.

With a flash, he crashes his lips against hers, sparks and warm tingles erupting between them. Juniper draws closer to Alec as they continue to kiss.

She finally takes a step back. 'I'm very sorry, sir. I'm not sure what got into me. I'd never openly kissed or desired to kiss a man like that before. So you'll have to forgive me,' she admits, blushing.

'What is your name?' he inquires.

'Juniper and yours, sir?'

'Alec,' he smiles. 'No need to apologise, Juniper. We are blood flames. Which means we are destined to be together,' he says.

'Blood flames?' She asks curiously.

Alec caresses her cheek, 'Yes, blood flames, when we touch it feels magical, like nothing else you’ve ever felt. Once we find each other, we have urges to stay close to each other. Staying away from each other causes pain and even death if not careful. We have been chosen to be together,’

'We are destined for each other?' she asks, taking a step closer to him.

'Yes,' he says, showing his fangs with a smile.

Juniper exhales and takes a step back. 'You've got fangs? And your eyes were red as fire when I first saw you?'

'That's because I'm not human,' he says quietly.

'You’re not human?' She pauses for a minute, then gasps once again. 'The creatures of the night, the ones who devour the blood from people and leave wounds on their necks?'

'Creatures of the night is one way to describe us, but we like the word vampire,' he smiles.

'Why are you killing people?' She asks.

'We survive by consuming blood. Human blood tastes the best, yet we drink from animals mostly to limit the number of human fatalities, and the people we kill are far from lovely people. This is because they have either raped, murdered or blackmailed people.

'I'm not human, either,' Juniper admits. 'I'm a witch, and the people in the valley are looking for me. 'So that's how I ended up here in the woods. If they discover me, they'll burn me at the stake, Alec,' she sobs as Alec draws her into his chest and consoles her.

'They can't hurt you if you stay with me, Juniper, my darling,' he says.

'I live with my grandmother in a cottage in the village over there. I need to see her. I need to take her with us,' she begs.

'Would it be too unsafe to return to the cottage?' Alec asks.

'I'll go at first light. Then, if there are no guards or men near the cottage, I will sneak in and get her,' Juniper says.

'Can't I grab her for you now while it's still dark?'

'The crowd will already be there, with lit torches and more men. I can't let them hurt you, Alec,' she says.

'I'm Alec, the vampire king, and I'll destroy them all before they blink,' he says, emanating a tremendous aura.

'Are you a King?' Juniper is taken aback.

'Yes, and you will be Queen,' he replies with admiration.

'You can't kill people, Alec. They are just terrified of witches. Once they realise we are harmless and only want to help them prosper and heal their sicknesses, they will cease hunting and burning us at the stake. Let's wait till the men have searched my grandmother's house. Then, when they realise I'm not there, they'll go, and we'll be able to take my grandmother and escape this place,'

'Wouldn't it be easier just to kill them?'

'I'm sure it would be Alec, but we're not monsters,' she replies, making Alec smile at the sweet, loving witch in front of him, knowing how fortunate he is that she was picked to be his blood flame.

Chapter 26

Alec and Juniper spend the night gazing up at the stars and moon as Alec learns everything he can about Juniper and her past.

'I think you should tell me more about yourself, Alec. I've been telling you everything about myself, but I still don't know anything about you other than you're Alec, the vampire King,' she replies enthusiastically.

'The sun will be rising soon, and I'm not fond of the day. We shall retrieve your grandma while it's still dark and return to my castle, where we will hold a great feast and celebrate our love. I will tell you all you want to know about me then,' he smiles.

Juniper nods, and they hold hands as they trudge through the woods to her village.

'Over there, that cottage there is where grandma and I live. I don't see anyone around, do you?' She asks.

Alec slowly and carefully scans the area, 'No, I don't see anyone,' he says.
'Stay here, I'll peep through the back window, and if no one is inside, I'll climb inside,'
'I'll keep watch outside then?' He says.

Juniper sneaks up to the window, peers through it, then turns and nods to Alec. Assuring him that everything is well on the inside. I hear her scream not long after she walks into the room. Alec bursts through the window inside the cottage, only to see men emerge from hiding. One man is holding a knife to the throat of an older woman, and I know it's her grandmother. Three men tackle juniper. Alec grabs one by the throat and throws the man out the window. The rest of the men stand around me, ready to fight. I hiss and bare my teeth, making them tremble.
'Creature of the night,' the grandmother murmurs.

Alec continues to kill them one by one.
More men enter the cabin as Juniper is dragged outside. She screams again when she sees the man with the knife slitting her grandmother's throat. Alec's hands emit a black mist as he summons Shadow Reapers and Grimghouls. The Grimghouls rip men apart, while Shadow Reapers

induce the men to imagine that other men are the enemy, and they begin attacking one other. Alec escapes the dwelling, only to find Juniper chained up to a wooden beam, standing on bundles of sticks. A man hurls a lit torch at her feet. 'No!' Alec yells and rushes towards her.

Men yell, 'Don't let him get to her, stop him!'

As Juniper screams in agony, Alec snaps their necks and rips the heads off dozens of men. As Alec approaches Juniper, her cries have stopped, and her entire body is enveloped in flames. She is no longer alive.

Alec's breathing becomes more rapid, and he sends out a high-pitched shriek that causes people's ears to bleed.

Thousands of black flashes zoom and dash around, moving too quickly to identify what they are, as people's limbs fly across the ground. Shrieks and screams are heard, and it quickly becomes silent. Finally, the black flashes come to a halt.

Hundreds of vampires stand near their king and watch him mourn his blood flame. They had killed everyone in the village. The only sound now is the cries coming from the king, the vampire king.

As the sun is about to rise and the fire is doused, he orders the vampires to retrieve Juniper's body for burial at the castle.

I am summoned to the Realm of Shadows alongside the Grimghouls and Shadow Reapers. We emerge at a gloomy medieval castle where the only light comes from a few candles spread about. Alec is standing over a dark stone coffin in the underground crypt. He lays black flowers upon it, kisses it, and walks out into the night. He raises his palms, and a burst of dark power emanates from all around him, opening a vast portal.

'I will avenge your death, Juniper, and all humans shall pay,' he cries into the night sky. Then, swarms of vampires, as well as Grimghouls and Shadow Reapers, rush through the portal. Alec is the last person to enter, and I rush in just as the portal closes.

We've arrived in werewolf territory. The alpha warns Alec to return to where he came from.

Alec laughs, 'You fool. I'm the vampire king. It is you who shall be warned. Join me and eradicate the humans or die along with them.'

The alpha charges at Alec but the Grimghouls shred him apart before he can even get near Alec.

The pack trembles and flees, informing other packs of what happened. Alec and his legion wiped out many packs over time that had tried to stop him from entering human lands and villages. A slew of witches appear and cast spells to keep Alec at bay.

'My blood flame was a witch. You should all be pursuing revenge alongside me!' Alec shouts.

The witches work together, casting spell after spell until he is encased in a magical whirl that prevents his entire body from moving. They create a portal, and on the other side, I can see the Midnight Coven. Alec is magically forced through the portal.

Other witches manage to contain the Grimghouls and Shadow Reapers and push them through to join their king. Alec continues to fight, but there are too many witches making him unable to repel all their spells at once. The swirls of magic around him lift him into the air and into the Covenstead.

A witch casts a spell in the corridor where two doors are. Her spell creates a third door, a new section of the Covenstead. She places a book in the room of darkness that forms into stairs and leads to a dark heavy door.

She opens it and casts another spell creating the dungeon. They confine the Grimghouls and Shadow Reapers to their cells and Alec to his. A witch draws a line of salt inside the iron-barred door, and several incantations are uttered. Alec is freed from the spell that had been binding him. He hisses and lunges at the bars and attempts to pass the line of salt.

His arm reaches through the line, and his arm spontaneously engulfs in flame, burning him. Alec falls back and pats his arm until the flames are out.

'It is of no use, vampire king. Your cell is bound by magic to keep you within. No matter your strength, you will never leave this cell until the day someone lets you out, but after wiping out most of the werewolf packs and intending to wipe out the human race. We sentence you to remain in this dungeon forever.' she says and walks away.

'No, come back. Please don't leave me here!' He screams out in agony.

The witches converse near the Shadow Reapers and Grimghouls.

'We have never seen these creatures before. I sense they are not what they seem,' Emmerson, a witch, says. Another pulls a mirror from her pocket and holds it in front of a Shadow Reaper. They gasp as they see the ghost of a human in the reflection.

'Try one of the Grimghouls,' Emmerson says. The mirror is held in front of a Grimghoul to reveal a pixie.

'The vampire King has summoned the souls of the dead and pixies from Silverfay forest and turned them into these hideous monsters.' She says to the other witches.

The witches begin to cast spells attempting to change them into their original states but fail. The Grimghouls and Shadow Reapers are a danger in these forms.

The witches have no choice but to keep them in the dungeon, hoping that a day will come when the pixies will be returned to Silverfay forest in their natural forms and the souls of the dead returned to their resting places.

As an added precaution, the witches inscribe sigils and lay wards over the doors after closing the heavy black door.

I'm suddenly pulled out of the dream state and back in real-time, looking into Alec's solemn eyes. I burst into tears and wrapped my arms around him, and cry.

‘I’m so sorry, Alec. I’m so sorry you lost your blood flame when you found her. I'm so sorry you've spent hundreds of years in here grieving her death and being alone,' I say.

'I'm sorry as well. I've spent a lot of time reflecting on her death and realised that she would not have wanted me to avenge her death. She was so kind that she would have wanted those guilty to survive, hoping that one day they would see their actions were wrong,' Alec says.

‘You shouldn’t be in here, in this dungeon. It’s not right to treat you like a-‘

‘Monster?’ He says, 'That's exactly what I became when Juniper died, Luna,'

'But you're not anymore,' I say as I gaze into his eyes.

Chapter 27

'Nina, please don't ask me again. We are not allowing Alec to leave that dungeon,' Magnus growls.

'If you saw what he showed me, how it all came about. You would see how unjust it is for him to remain in there,' I say.

'Nina, I would never put myself in that position in the first place. Your blood flame made his choice, and he now suffers the consequences,'

'If I was burned at the stake, would you not try and kill those responsible?' I ask.

Magnus stiffens, and instead of responding, he walks away upstairs to our room and slams the door.

With Reaper on my shoulder, I sigh and stroll over to the open window.

'That didn't go down well,' Reaper mind-links.

'Well, it's a complicated situation for Magnus, he is my mate, and the vampire king is my second mate,'

'Did you hear that, Reaper?' I ask as I hear a gasp from the garden.

'Yes,' he says and flies from my shoulder and circles through the garden, searching.

'Who's there?' I shout out the window. 'Come out now, and I might let you live,' I crack my knuckles and climb out the window. When Reaper lets out a caw, I know he's located something... or someone. So I take a step forward and tackle the person.

'Don't kill me, please don't kill me,' Hank begs.

'Hank? What are you doing in my territory? You were exiled from here. You were never supposed to return,' I growl.

'I came to ah, apologise, yes apologise and make amends for my… terrible behaviour trying to blackmail Magnus into a mateship with my sister,' he says in a higher-pitched voice.

'You know I have every right to kill you for returning and trespassing?'

'Y-yes,' he says, falls to his knees, and bows before me, 'But you are such a kind, understanding Luna. Would you really kill someone for trying to right their wrong?' He says, making me think of Juniper and how she would have wanted Alec to forgive the humans. I frown in thought. My gut is telling me to kill him, right here, right now. But my heart is thinking of Alec and Magnus and what would be the right thing to do.

He looks up to see my outreached hand and takes it to stand up. 'Thank you, Luna,' he says.

'What were you doing in the garden anyway? Why didn't you just knock at the packhouse door?'

'Um, I thought if Magnus or someone else were to greet me at the door, they would not be as understanding as you would be and kill me without hearing me out first,' he explains.

'I see,' I say.

'Now that you have heard what I have to say and accepted my sincerest apologies, I will be on my way then,' He says, taking his leave.

'Wait, how come I can't smell your scent? The warriors should have known you were here,' I say.

Hank fondles a symbol made from a precious stone around his neck. He doesn't know what to say. I step forward and hold the symbol and take a closer look. 'I've seen this symbol before,' I say, trying to think of where I have seen it. I yank it from his neck, turn my back to him, and hold it up for Reaper to see. 'Wasn't this mentioned in one of the spellbooks? I'm pretty sure it hides your scent?'

'Yes, that's an excellent observation,' Reaper mind-links. I return my attention to Hank, but he has already left.

'Something odd about that, Hank,' I say.

'Are you going to chase after him?' Reaper mind-links.

'No, I need to check on Magnus,'

Reaper flies over me and onto the railing outside my bedroom window, readying himself to eavesdrop on our conversation. Rolling my eyes at him, I enter the packhouse and 'Skedaddle Dash' upstairs and knock on the bedroom door.

I hear a grunt which I take as a sign to enter. Magnus sits on the end of the bed with his head down. Instead of saying anything, I sit on his lap and snuggle into him. He immediately relaxes and wraps his arms tightly around me.

'I'm sorry,' I whisper.

'I know, I am too,'

We stay embraced silently in each other's arms for a while.

'I should finish off the paperwork in the office. Do you want to come with me?' Magnus asks.

'I think I'll go down to the basement and socialise with my coven sisters,' I smile.

Entering the basement, there is a new large circular table with wooden seats that have carvings.

'This table is beautiful,' I exclaim to Ela, Fern, Lilac, Ria and May.

'We materialised it together. It's just for us witches for meetings and other such things,' May says.

I notice the back of each chair has a name. I take the seat with Luna written in gold on the back. It's very comfortable. 'Well, we could utilise it right now. I have something I want you all to know,'

Everyone stops brewing the potion and takes their seat.

'What is it, Luna?' Fern asks.

'Alec showed me what had happened to Juniper, his first blood flame, and why he attempted to wipe out the human race. I want you to all know his story. I'm going to tell you what I saw in the vision he showed me,'

'Wait a minute. We have a vision spell as well. Please allow me to get the book for you.' Ela remarks as she walks over to the spellbook rack.

She flips over the pages, places the book in front of me, and retakes her seat. When I look down at the paper and pronounce the words, 'Visionous Memorias,' a great circle of magic appears and shows what I'm thinking about. I start where Alec left off, with Juniper rushing down the cobblestone path, entering the cottage, putting the healing potions in her basket, and departing to give the potion to the Hillsburys.

When the vision is finished, everyone is wailing and crying, their eyes downcast. Behind me, I hear a shuffle towards the stairs. Magnus had witnessed the entire vision, and tears streamed down his cheeks. I dash over to him and give him a tight embrace. He gently squeezes me back.

'That was... incredibly difficult to watch,' Magnus says quietly.

I wipe the tears from his face and turn to face the others. They are crying into their familiars. Sabre, the fennec fox whimpers as he licks May's tears from her face.

'It's so sad,' May sniffles, 'Alec never even got to spend a whole day with Juniper, and she was killed before his very own eyes,'

'And Juniper never got to take her grandma back to Alec's castle,' Fern cries.

'They killed her grandma,' Ria cries.

I take Magnus's hand, and we walk upstairs and out of the packhouse and sit under the moon tree.

Reaper caws and flies down from the tree onto the grass for a pat.

'I can see why you think it's unfair that Alec is still in that dungeon, but it's also for the best,' Magnus says.

'Are you kidding me? It's for the best?'

'Let's say we let him out, Nina. What do you think he is going to do? Prance around and pick flowers from the garden? No, I'm your mate, which means he will want me out of the picture and will probably attempt to kill me or succeed and kill me,'

'He wouldn't,' I say.

'Are you willing to stake my life on that, Nina?'

Would Alec murder Magnus if we let him out of the dungeon? I'd never considered it before.

'If Alec truly loves me, Magnus, he would never do anything to hurt me, and if that means you staying alive and being by my side, then I'm sure that is something he will accept and adjust to,' I say.

'I need to let my wolf out for a run. I'll see you tonight.' He says and shifts into his wolf, bolting towards the woods.

Chapter 28

Alpha Bennet taps his fingers repetitively in the dark of night. Alpha Amir and Alpha Theaton sit at the table beside him. The candelabra above them only dimly lights the room. Hank brings a large jug of wine to the table and refills everyone's cups before taking a seat himself.

'How much longer do we have to wait for this Kadva you speak of to arrive?' Hank asks, evidently impatient with waiting.

The window shutters suddenly blow open, candles flicker, and the lace curtain dances in the air before settling itself back down.

Hank looks towards the window to see no one there but becomes startled when he sees a hooded figure on the seat beside him.

'What in the world!' Hank says, 'Where did you come from?'

'Kadva, it's nice of you to join us,' Alpha Bennet says.

'It's been a while, Alpha Bennet,' Kadva says, sounding polite.

'Something interesting has occurred and in our favour too,' Alpha Bennet smiles.

'Oh?' Kadva says as he turns his hand upright, and a blue orb of magic appears. He bounces it up and down in his hand as if bored.

Hank's eyes grow wide, 'What is that thing?' he says, frantically pointing at Kadva.

The wolf council are calm, as if it's normal for them to see such magic.

'Hank, this is Kadva. He is a mage,' Alpha Bennet says, almost too calm.

'A M-mage? I never knew such a thing existed,' Hank says.

Kadva turns his head at Hank, 'Refer to me as a thing again, Hank, and maybe I will show you what this thing is capable of,' Kadva grits through his teeth.

Hank stiffens and goes silent.

'Let's get back to business, Kadva. We agreed many years ago that we would keep you a secret from society so you could live your life free from being hunted down by humans. In return, you would owe us a big favour if we ever needed it. That time is now,' Alpha Bennet smirks.

'I'm listening,' Kadva says.

'We all have mutual feelings toward the human race and find it unfair that we have to stay hidden from humans, century after century.

We have even joked about wiping them out, but for thousands of werewolves to go up against billions of humans and their weapons of destruction. We know it would never be possible, and we would lose.

However, there is a pack we have disliked for some time now, Shadow Crest.

They are responsible for killing alpha Zenith many years ago and, more recently, his daughter Vanessa and grandson Moss. As you know, Alpha Zenith used to be a part of this council, and we were practically brothers.

Now Alpha Magnus has taken over the pack, and it turns out his little mate is half-witch,'

'What? That's impossible,' Kadva says, 'There hasn't been a record of a witch in hundreds of years,'

'There is no record of a mage either,' Alpha Bennet smiles, 'But yet, here you are. It gets even better from here. A coven of witches came forward and made themselves known to Shadow Crest,'

'There are more? What is the coven called?' Kadva asks.

'The Midnight Coven or something along those lines. They made Nina, and her sister, who also wields magic, members of their coven and then the coven were also welcomed into the Shadow Crest pack,'

'One big happy family,' Kadva chuckles. 'But I can see how that would be a problem to you and all other packs. They would stand out having witches and magic on their side, making them the most powerful pack to exist,'

'Yes, it is a problem, a big problem. We went to see them and Yiselda, the coven leader, spoke about how they are needed to protect Pandora's Box from opening.

That it holds beings from your worst nightmares and would wipe all species from the earth, including us, if ever freed.

I asked to see this Pandora's Box, and Yiselda refused. We gave the witches, including their precious Luna, a day to vanish from any pack territories and never return. Otherwise, we would hunt them down and kill them. We left, and further along the road, this smouldering blackbird gave me a note to come back the next day, where I would be taken to Pandora's Box.

We returned the next day and entered a portal with the witches. It was their Covenstead which they named Pandora's Box. I entered the house to find items floating and moving around. We stepped through a large mirror and opened a door that led to darkness. Yiselda made a staircase magically appear using a book, and then we walked up the stairs until we reached a large dark heavy door covered in sigils.

It was a dungeon, we entered, and the first hideous creatures I saw were what they call Grimghouls. Then there were the Shadow Reapers further up. They were all interesting creatures, but what got my attention was the lone vampire king locked away in a small dark cell,'

'The vampire king?' Kadva says as he drops his ball of magic onto the table. It shatters into light blue glimmering dust, scattering across the table.

'So not only do witches still exist but Grimghouls, Shadow Reapers and vampires too?

And not just any vampire, the vampire king?' Kadva says.

'Yes, hundreds of years ago, humans killed his blood flame, who happened to be a witch. He created the Grimghouls and Shadow Reapers to try and help save her. Afterwards, he sent them across the lands to kill all humans. Werewolf packs teamed up and tried to stop him. He wiped out most of the packs until witches intervened and have kept him in the dungeon ever since.'

'This is all rather interesting to hear. After all these years, I thought werewolves and myself were the only supernatural creatures left?'

'Well, the story gets more interesting again. I've had Hank here wear that necklace you gave me years ago to cover scents and sent him to spy on Shadow Crest. He returned with rather intriguing news. It turns out Nina, the half-wolf and half-witch Luna, isn't only mates with Magnus but is also mates with the vampire king,'

'They have the vampire king on their side as well?' Kadva says, astonished at the thought.

'Not quite, Nina wants to let him out, but the others are against it, especially Alpha Magnus,'

'Well, I'm intrigued as to where I fit in all of this and still not sure where you are going with all this information?'

'I want the humans gone, wiped out, non-existent, and we can now achieve that with the vampire king's help. We can take over the world and never have to hide. A human free world full of werewolves!' Alpha Bennet Beams.

Kadva awkwardly coughs.

'Oh, supernatural's, I guess I should say?' He corrects himself.

'And how do you supposed we achieve that? We don't know how to get to the vampire king and if he will want to wipe out the human species?' Kadva says.

'Actually,' Hank interrupts, 'I happened to follow them through a portal to Pandora's Box and was able to figure out the location. It's a few hours run in wolf form from here,' he smirks and folds his arms.

'We are not going to visit the vampire king and just ask him if he would do it. We will make him do it. You, Kadva, will take Nina's wand and kidnap her. Magnus will notice her missing. You will leave this note telling him in order to have Nina safely returned, he needs to free the vampire king, and the vampire king needs to eradicate the human race,'

'So, I'm to remove Nina's wand removing her of magic, kidnap her, leave this note and have Nina hidden and locked up somewhere until there are no humans alive?'

'Correct,' Alpha Bennet says, 'Except we won't be handing Nina over. I want the witches and that vampire dead as well. Hank will burn Pandora's Box down. We will kill the witches, and together we will kill the vampire king,'

'Are you sure you want all the blood of those humans and witches on your hand? It doesn't feel right just to wipe them out. What if we can't kill the vampire king?'

We will seal him in a dungeon for eternity using Nina's magic and then kill her. If you refuse to cooperate, Kadva, tell me now because I'm sure the humans would love to hear all about this mage that can manipulate elements, they would like to get their hands on. As well as lock-up in one of those laboratories and be experimented on every day?' Alpha Bennet warns.

Kadva stiffens, 'So when do I leave for Shadow Crest?' He asks.

'Tonight.' Alpha Bennet smiles.

Chapter 29

The entire town of Shadow Crest has been abuzz with rumours about the vampire king being my second mate. We'll be having Astrid, Ryker, and my parents around for dinner to talk about it all in more detail.

The moment they walk into the packhouse, we all meet and embrace one another, 'Please take a seat in the dining room. It won't be long until dinner is served.' I smile.

The kitchen staff have laid out a feast along the table, and we have begun to pile food onto our plates.

'So, dear, tell me all about the vampire king? Does he treat you well? Is he handsome?' My Mum inquires.

'Amelia!' Magnus says with a snarl.

'What? I think we're all a little curious,' she says.

‘You asked Nina about her second mate in such a casual manner, as if it were entirely common to have two mates,’ Magnus says.

'Well, it's quite natural. In my childhood, my grandmother had two mates, and another pack member had two female mates as well. I remember my grandmother giggling her way from one bedroom to the other in the middle of the night,' Amelia recalls fondly.

Magnus is dumbfounded and looks at his parents for guidance and comfort.

'Actually, son,' Ryker adds, taking a bite of roast beef in his mouth, 'Amelia is absolutely correct. My grandmother had two mates, as did her cousin, who also had two mates. In fact, most packs had at least one or two members who were blessed with two soulmates,' he says with a smirk.

'And they were completely okay with that? Sharing their mate?' Magnus asks, completely taken aback.

‘Well yeah, Nina isn’t just your mate. She is also the vampire king’s mate. What’s his name anyway?’ Ryker asks.

‘Alec,’ Magnus grizzles, clenching the fork in his hand tighter. 'I have no intention of sharing Nina with him, and she is just visiting him once a day until we can figure out how to break the bond between them,' Magnus explains.

The cutlery clatters and crashes against the plates and everyone's eyes are drawn to Magnus in surprise.

'Mate, relationships are sacred. They should never be broken,' Ryker asserts firmly.

'Nina is mine!' Magnus lets out a growl.

'She is Alec's as well, Magnus. Would you like him to keep Nina away from you every day and try to sever your mate bond with her?' My dad, Leon, argues.

Magnus clenches his teeth at the concept, 'No,' he says.

'Take a moment to consider what you are doing to Alec. He is Nina's, second mate. Whatever you do to him will cause Nina sorrow, and anything he does to hurt you will also cause Nina suffering,' Leon says.

'What are you saying? I should be mutual with Alec and share Nina with him?' Magnus laughs.

'Well, if you want what is best for your mate, then yes,' Leon says.

'Has it not sunk in at this point that Nina's second mate isn't even a werewolf? He is a vampire, and he is the king of the vampires!' Magnus argues.

'Nina's extremely lucky, an alpha and a king,' Amelia says, smiling as Nina blushes in response.

'I'm out of here,' Magnus says as he rises from his seat at the table and proceeds toward the packhouse door.

'So, sweetheart, you didn't respond to my queries,' my mother says with a smile.

'He is quite sweet and gentle towards me, Mum. He is as equally attractive as Magnus is,'

'Don't worry about Magnus. He will come around. I forget with fewer packs now. It has become more uncommon over time to see anyone with two mates. He wouldn't be taking it so hard if he had known earlier how common and natural it was back when we were young,' Ryker says.

'Do you all really think Alec and Magnus would eventually become mutual?' I ask. Everyone smiles and nods their heads.

'The fact that Magnus is opposed to releasing Alec from the dungeon means that it is unlikely to happen for a long time,' I explain.

Magnus returns to the table, where he silently continues his meal.

'Back so soon?' I smile.

'Well, I didn't have much of a choice. Reaper kept trying to swoop me,' he grumbles.

I laugh and lean over to embrace him with my arms around his waist.

We complete our dinner without saying anything about Alec, and then we escort our parents out of the packhouse together.

'I'm going to tell Reaper off for swooping you,' I say.

'I'll meet you upstairs for bed,' Magnus replies and places a kiss on my forehead.

As I walk closer to the moon tree, I call out, 'Reaper,' He flies down and lands on my shoulder. 'Can you tell me why you were swooping, Magnus?'

'Because I could sense he was upsetting you during dinner,' he explains.

'I have the ability to fight my own battles, Reaper. Please don't swoop him anymore, okay?'

'I'm your familiar Luna, and we work as a team. It's my responsibility to watch out for you,' he says with a squawk. 'However, I'll make an effort not to swoop him the next time he offends you,'

'You know, you never ended up telling me how you and Alec know each other?'

'I haven't lived my entire life in Silverfay forest. I enjoy venturing out into the world to explore what has changed since I was last there. I was resting in the woods one night when I was roused by Alec sprinting past the tree in front of me. He cornered a deer and buried his teeth into its neck to bring it down.

I watched as he drank the blood till he finally fell to his knees, looking relieved. He looked around, sensing that something was wrong, and realised he was being watched. He stood up, turned around, and looked right at me perched on the branch. If you can cast me the vision spell, I will show you the rest,'

'Visionous Memorias,' I say, a large clear circle of magic appears, and I see Alec staring at Reaper in the tree.

'You aren't an ordinary raven,' Alec says through a mind-link.

'No, I'm not,' Reaper replies to Alec.

'What is a familiar doing roaming the world? Shouldn't you be in Shadowfay forest with the rest of your kind?' Alec asks.

'I'm not like the other familiars. I'm the only Shadow Raven to exist. I'm more powerful than any other familiar, and I was bored,' Reaper says.

'The most powerful familiar, bored?' Alec laughs.

'Watching pixies prance around, tossing magic dust all over the place, all day, every day,' Reaper admits, 'Can be a little tedious,'

Alec continues to laugh, 'I suppose it would be. What's your name, bird?' Alec asks.

'Reaper, and yours?'

'Alec, Vampire King,' he proclaims with pride.

'What is a vampire king doing in these desolate woods?' Reaper asks.

'I was on the verge of going mad. I needed to get some nourishment quickly before I lost my senses. These woodlands are lifeless and devoid of any form of life. With the exception of you, this deer is the first living creature I have seen in several days.' Alec explains.

Reaper descends from the tree, a dark cloud of mist enveloping him as he falls on Alec's shoulder.

'That was a brave move, my little friend. Are you not afraid I will sink my teeth into you and take your life?' Alec asks.

Reaper caws and stretches his wings, 'No, you just drained the blood from an entire deer. I'm confident you are quite full,' he says. 'So, Alec, Vampire King. Now that you have your senses back, where are we off to?'

'My home, the Realm of Shadows.' He says as he and Reaper flash through the woods together.

Chapter 30

The magic vision circle fades.

'Did you spend a lot of time with Alec?' I ask Reaper.

'A few hundred years till the witches imprisoned him in that dungeon. Juniper was murdered in front of my eyes. I saw everything. Because I wasn't his familiar, I couldn't pass on my powers to him. I couldn't follow him through the portal to Pandora's Box.

The witches kept repelling me back with magic. It closed before I reached it. After years of searching for Alec, I returned to Silverfay forest and remained there until you arrived,'

'I'm so sorry, Reaper. That's a lot for anyone to go through,' I grimace.

I smile and say, 'When we visit Alec tomorrow, I'll give you two some alone time to talk and catch up,'

'I'd like that,' says Reaper. For a while, we sit and gaze at the moon. 'Goodnight, Reaper,' I reply, kissing his beak.

'Night, Luna,' he caws as he flies up into his moon tree.

I walk to the lake, not quite ready to retire to bed, tucking my wand into my back pocket, half poking out. I lie on my back, hands tucked behind my head, and gaze up at the stars in the clear night sky.

Something flitters through the air. It appeared to be a little stone.

I sit up, perplexed, as someone sneaks up behind me and grabs the wand from my back pocket. A hand grabs my arm and pulls it behind my back as I turn around. A knee digs into my back, causing me to fall to my knees, then on my stomach. I scream, but whoever it is, has straddled themselves onto my back, and I hear a man's voice 'Dreamus Sleepous,' he says, and I fall asleep.

As I open my eyes, everything appears fuzzy. My tied wrists and the hard brick wall against my back are the first things I notice. I'm seated on a cold stone floor that's cold to the touch. Then, as my vision sharpens, I realise I'm in an old jail-like cell. I try to mind-link Magnus right away, but nothing happens. The mind-link connection has been severed. I try to untangle my hands, but the rope tightens.

Take a deep breath, Nina, and stay calm. Let us examine the situation. I've obviously been kidnapped and am now imprisoned in a cell. My wand has been stolen, so I can't utilise my magic and can't mind-link anyone, not even Magnus. I don't believe I've sustained any injuries.

I wiggle around to see if I can feel any pain or injuries; nope, no pain, no injuries other than from the rope burn around my wrists.

Now the question is, who would kidnap me, and why would they do so? I can't conceive of anyone who would want to do this to me, so I concentrate on chewing the rope around my wrists and spitting out the tiny prickly fibres.

Footsteps are approaching. I gaze up to see the wolf council and Hank looking at me with smug expressions. Someone else is lurking behind them, a hooded figure.

'Alpha Bennet, what am I here? Why did you kidnap me?

'Welcome, Luna. I see you've settled comfortably in your cell,' Alpha Bennet chuckles.

I scoff, 'Comfortably is far from the term I would use! Now answer my question!' I shout.

'So, dramatic,' Alpha Bennet says, 'And I didn't kidnap you for starters. Kadva did,'

'Who is Kadva?' I ask.

The hooded figure stepped forward. He held his hands out, and they began to glow. A blue magic sphere appears in both of his hands and transforms into balls of water.

'I'm Kadva,' he introduces himself.

'How did you manage to do that? Who are you?' I ask, astounded by his powers.

'Kadva is a mage,' Alpha Bennet interrupts the conversation.

'A mage? My coven sisters would really love to meet you, well, before you kidnapped me, of course, but I'm sure they'd want to meet you for less than pleasant reasons now,' I frown.

'I'm just following orders,' Kadva says in defence.

'Following orders? You work for the wolf council?'

'The one and only,' he says in an uncomfortable manner.

Despite the fact that Kadva kidnapped me, I can't help but think he's not really an evil guy. I'm curious about what they have against Kadva to force him to do their bidding.

'I'm not sure why I'm here. Why did you have me kidnapped?' I look up at Alpha Bennet.

'How would you feel if this planet was free of humans? To live in a world where we are no longer required to keep our powers hidden. To be able to shift into our wolves without being hunted down and slaughtered by humans?'

'This planet was made for humans. It was never intended to have supernaturals on it in the first place. Books dating back a thousand years can be found in the Shadow Crest library's forbidden room. I read one book in particular. It documents the history of supernaturals.

We did not come from here but from another dimension called Mysteria. To answer your question, I would not feel right if humans no longer existed, especially in their own world where they are meant to be. I prefer to leave the humans alone and return to Mysteria if given a choice. But I'm not sure what my kidnapping and confinement here has to do with this?'

Alpha Bennet bursts into laughter, 'You were supposed to say how wonderful living in a human-free world would be. Your priority should be for your own species. You're a disgrace to all werewolves.'

I jump to my feet and lunge at the bars where Alpha Bennet stands, 'You're lucky I don't have my wand and that I'm behind these bars. The wolf council is the disgrace!' I shout.

Alpha Theaton laughs. 'And the Luna hasn't even heard the best part yet,'

'What part?' I ask, knowing I'm not going to like what I hear next.

'The part where Magnus will never see you again until your blood flame the vampire king wipes out the human race,' Alpha Theaton grins.

'H-He won't do it!' I yell.

'Oh, but he will. He was going to do it once to revenge his first blood flame, and if he wants you back, he will have no choice but to proceed with annihilating the human race,'

I glare at Hank, 'This is why you were back in Shadow Crest? You were spying on me? How else would the wolf council know that Alec is my blood-flame?'

Hank smiles proudly at himself, 'You should have killed me when you had the chance,' he laughs.

'Oh, don't you worry, Hank, the next opportunity I get, I will kill you,' I warn. He stiffens and stops laughing.

I lower my gaze, concentrate, and try to mind-link Reaper, Magnus, and anyone else from my pack, but nothing happens. I glare up at Kadva.

'You did something to sever my mind-linking ability, didn't you?'

Although I can't see his face under his hood, I can sense he is highly uncomfortable. He remains silent but nods.

'Please, Kadva, I have to tell Magnus not to free Alec. I don't want the human race to die because of me. My life is not worth the death of billions of innocent people!' I plead.

Kadva doesn't reply and walks away.

'I have to agree with you, Luna. Your insignificant life is not worth the life of even one human being. But both of your lovers will think otherwise, so sit tight, sweetheart, because the world is about to change,' he says, laughing along with Alpha Theaton and Alpha Amir. They walk away.

'You'll be sorry!' You will all be sorry! Please, no one should die!' I yell at the top of my lungs through the bars.

They slam the door shut behind them, and I drop to the ground, hugging my knees. I need to get out of here, and I need to put a stop to this.

I chew through the rope until it's frail enough to snap. Then, with my hands now free, I slowly and thoroughly inspect every inch of the cell for any flaw or vulnerability through which I can escape.

Chapter 31

Magnus wakes up through the night to discover that Nina has not yet gone to bed. He peers out the window to check if Nina is still by the moon tree. There's no trace of her.

'I can't smell her scent,'

'Nina?' He shouts as he walks down the hallway and then down the stairwell. Lilac and May are the first ones to leave their bedrooms.

'Alpha Magnus, it's like three o'clock in the morning. Why are you shouting?' Lilac asks, adding a yawn.

'Have any of you seen Nina?' He asks, 'She didn't come to bed with me last night,'

'When was the last time you saw her?' May inquires.

'She was under the moon tree with Reaper. I'll go wake him up and ask him if he knows where she has disappeared to. Not that he can tell me, but perhaps he can show me.'

As Magnus approaches the moon tree, he notices Reaper, fast asleep with his beak tucked beneath one of his wings.

'Reaper, Reaper, I need you to wake up.'

Reaper stirs awake, stretches his wings, and clicks his beak.

'Nina didn't come to bed last night. Do you know where she went? Can you show me where she has gone?'

Reaper begins to caw and screech in response to this. He seems troubled that Nina isn't here. As he searches for her, he takes to the sky. I shift into my wolf and run after him.

He will have a better field of vision than I will, flying in the air. Nina may have been injured and might be unable to move. It would explain why she never came home, but she didn't mind-link me. I try to mind-link her, but the connection is gone.

Reaper makes his way into town. I shift back and inspect the forbidden room, but she isn't there. After that, we head to the lake. 'She was here at some time throughout the night. I can smell her scent.' I say to Reaper as we look around.

As I approach the lake, I notice a rock that has been weirdly positioned near the water. I see a note under the rock and pick it up. Reaper takes flight and settles on my shoulder as I raise the note up to show him.

'Alpha Magnus, if you want your precious Luna returned alive, you are to free the vampire king, and he is to eradicate the human race. Once the human race has been annihilated, that's when your Luna will be returned. If you both refuse this order, then we will kill her, and then we will destroy your entire pack declaring you an enemy to all wolf packs and kill every single pack member.

Regards,

The Wolf Council'

Reaper squawks and flies around in a crazy manner across the air. While I fall to my knees in shock and in response to the ultimatum that has been placed before me, I raise my eyes to the sky.

'Luna, I will get you back one way or another. I will bring you back home safe where you belong. I promise you.'

Magnus shifts and returns to the packhouse. Reaper perches on his shoulder. The sun is just beginning to rise in the sky. Everyone is already awake and alert after May and Lilac awoke the entire packhouse to notify them that Nina has gone missing.

'Has anyone been able to mind-link Nina?' Magnus asks. May attempts to mind-link her.

'There is nothing,' May says in dismay.

Magnus approaches the witches, drinking tea at the table, 'I need you to take me to Pandora's Box. I need to speak with Alec,' he says.

'Why Alec? Wouldn't Yiselda be a better help?' Fern asks.

Magnus holds the note up, 'The wolf Council have taken Nina hostage. They left a note for Alec and me,'

'What!' May shouts.

'What does it say?' Ela asks.

'I will tell you what it all says later. But, for now, I need to speak with Alec, so Nina can be returned safe and alive,' he says, knowing too well that if the witches know there is a chance that Magnus will let Alec out, then they most likely won't allow him into Pandora's Box again.

'All right, we can go now.' The rest of the witches and I follow Ela as she proceeds to the portal, where we enter through the circle and emerge outside Pandora's Box. After entering the coven stead, I walk towards the giant mirror until Lilac lays her hand on my back and tells me to stop.

'Alpha Magnus, we need to tell Yiselda first that Nina has been kidnapped and that you need to speak to Alec urgently,' she says.

'We'll inform her afterwards,' Magnus says.

'Sorry, Alpha Magnus, but you will have to follow me into the kitchen and see Yiselda,' Lilac says. Magnus, annoyed, clenches the note.

'Fine!' He snaps and follows them into the kitchen.

'Yiselda, something terrible has happened!' May says, racing over to Yiselda, who is eating breakfast.

'What is it?' She says, startled, standing up.

'Luna, she has been kidnapped by the wolf council. They left a note for Magnus and Alec,'

'What does it say?' Yiselda asks.

'You may read it once I've spoken to Alec,' Magnus says, masking his displeasure at the question. ' It's important that I speak with him right away. Nina is in danger,' he says.

Yiselda stares intently at Magnus for a brief moment. 'Well, I better take you to him then,' she says and leads the way out of the kitchen and through the mirror. She materialises a book and transforms it into a stairway, and everyone follows her up to the enormous, hefty door in the distance. Yiselda unlocks the door, and Magnus dashes by her, ignoring the Grimghouls and Shadow Reapers he passes along the way.

'Alec, Alec,' Magnus shouts. He looks up to see two glowing brown eyes in the shadows of the cell.

'I know you, and I aren't close for obvious reasons, but Nina is gone. The Wolf Council have kidnapped her,'

Alec comes face to face with Magnus with such speed, sending Magnus to tumble back to the ground.

'What do you mean the wolf council has kidnapped her? Nina is a witch, and she has her wand. So, she would be able to protect herself.' Alec says.

Alec is right. Even with all three alphas up against her, they still would not have been able to kidnap her.

The witches have caught up and circle the cell listening to our conversation.

'I'm not lying. The wolf council must have had help to kidnap her,' Magnus says as he hands Alec the note. 'Perhaps they were able to take her wand away from her?'

'That would make sense if what you say is true,' Alec says, accepting the note. He holds it up and reads it out loud.

'Alpha Magnus, if you want your precious Luna returned alive, you are to free the vampire king, and he is to eradicate the human race. Once the human race has been annihilated, that's when your Luna will be returned. If you both refuse this order, then we will kill her, and then we will destroy your entire pack declaring you an enemy to all wolf packs and kill every single pack member.

Regards,

The Wolf Council'

The witches gasp and whisper amongst each other. Alec's breathing becomes heavy, and he looks away in shock.

'They have my blood flame and took her away from me. I will make the wolf council pay!' Alec viciously hisses and lets out a horrendous deafening screech, with his hands clenched around the bars. Magnus and the witches cover their ears. The Grimghouls have become louder, hissing and snarling while the Shadow Reapers shriek. Alec locks eyes with Magnus.

'You have to let me out. Let me save Nina.'

Before Magnus can respond, Yiselda steps closer.

'Not going to happen… ever.' She says sternly.

Chapter 32

'Alpha Magnus, I hope you weren't intending on letting Alec out? Is that why you wanted us to remain unaware of the note's contents?' Yiselda asks.

Reaper squawks furiously at her before flying from Magnus's shoulder and walking through the bars, perching on Alec's shoulder.

Alec scratches Reaper's beak and pats him, much to Yiselda's bewilderment.

'In all honesty, Yiselda, I had no idea whether I would release him or not, but I came prepared, for if I do. All I know is that I need Nina back in my arms and if we can't come up with any other alternative, then....'

'Stop! You will not go there, Alpha Magnus,' Yiselda growls. 'I know Nina is your mate and Luna, but we can't allow the humans to be wiped out in her place,'

'Yes, we can,' Alec interrupts, 'Now let me out!'

'Repeliate,' Yiselda says, waving her wand at Alec. He is thrown backwards by Yiselda's magic against the cell's back wall. 'I will not let you harm the humans,' she says.

'What do you suppose we do then, Yiselda?' Magnus asks.

'Nothing, we do nothing,' she says.

'And let Nina, your Luna and coven sister perish?'

'Her death will not go unnoticed. Do you believe I desire Luna's demise? No! However, we cannot allow billions of people to perish in order to save her. Do you believe she would desire that?' Yiselda refutes.

Magnus stiffens and clenches his hands as they begin to tremble. 'I can't live without her. If you are unable to come up with a better plan, then it will leave me with no choice but to release Alec,'

Yiselda pauses in thought and turns to Alec and asks, 'After all these years, you still wish to eradicate humankind to avenge your blood flame?'

'If I could travel back in time, Yiselda, I would change everything. I'm relieved that I was unable to eradicate humanity. Juniper would not have wanted me to destroy them, and I regret killing anybody who attempted to stop me. If I had been released before Nina's kidnapping, I would not have sought revenge. It hasn't been easy, but I've recognised Juniper is no longer with us and that killing humans would not bring her back.

Meeting Nina and having her as my second chance blood flame means the world to me right now. My primary concern is to keep her safe, alive, and close to me. I know Nina wouldn't want me to eradicate the humans either, but the difference between Juniper and Nina is that Juniper is dead and Nina is alive. I would do anything to keep Nina alive,'

'I'm sorry, Alec. I can't let you out, knowing you will kill the humans. It is final,' Yiselda says.

'Not, if I have a say in it,' Magnus says, crossing his arms.

'Alpha Magnus, I have no choice but to ask you to leave,' Yiselda says.

'Oh, I'm going to leave, but I'm going to take Alec with me,'

Alec shakes his head in bewilderment at Magnus, unable to believe what he is hearing.

'I can't allow you to do that, Alpha. Please don't force me to use magic against you.' Yiselda cautions, removing her wand.

'You won't have to,' Alpha Magnus says.

Alec and the witches exchange puzzled glances. Yiselda flutters her wand in preparation to cast a spell. Magnus growls, in his Alpha tone, 'Yield and lay down your wands,'

All the witches instantly lay down their wands and kneel, except for May.

'How is this possible?' Yiselda asks, concerned.

'You became a member of my pack. All alphas have the power to subdue any of their members,' he smiles.

'Unbelievable,' Alec says, wedging his head against the bars. 'Guess you didn't see that one coming, Yiselda?' Alec grins.

No, I did not,' she states angrily.

'Magnus, are you sure about this?' May asks.

'Is there any other option?'

May's shoulders slump in defeat, and she nods her head no.

Magnus moves by Yiselda and takes a position in front of the cell door.

'Alpha Magnus, I beg you, please don't let him out. He will kill us all,' Yiselda warns.

Alec steps towards the cell door, anxious for his freedom, but keeps behind the salt line, knowing that attempting to pass it would be harmful.

'Alec, there is something I need to do before I release you,' Magnus says as he draws out the athame, the identical one used in the witches' initiation ceremony.

Yiselda is confused that Magnus has a knife and wonders if he is going to harm Alec with it.

Alec scowls at Magnus, 'If you believe you're going to knife me, you're in for a surprise. I could kill you before you unsheathe it,' he says.

'Relax, Alec. As much as I would like to stab you, Nina would never forgive me, so you can dismiss that thinking. This is not an easy decision for me to make, but with Nina's life on the line, I have no option but to initiate you into my pack,' Magnus explains.

Alec blinks a few times and bursts into laughter. 'Me? Join your pack?'

'Remember, it's not only my pack. It's also Nina's,' Magnus says.

Alec stops laughing, 'You're being serious?'

'You can't be serious?' May and Yiselda say in unison.

'A vampire in our pack?' Fern stutters.

'Alec, I need assurance that you will not harm Yiselda or the other witches and that you will not do something silly like flee with Nina and keep her to yourself,' Magnus says.

'Fine!' Alec sighs deeply. You have my assurance. I will not attack the witches except in self-defence, and I will not kidnap Nina for my own selfish reasons...' he huffs.

'I need more than your word Alec. I need your initiation into the pack,' Magnus states.

'No, you want me to join the pack just so you may exert power over me in the manner of the witches,' he shouts.

'That is true. Nonetheless, it is for your own benefit. You will be incapable of harming any pack members this way,'

'I'm a king, and I don't take orders from anyone!' Alec yells.

'And you will still be King of all vampires. Your status won't change. Submitting into the pack verifies everyone's safety, including yours.'

Alec turns his head to Reaper on his shoulder. They seem to be mind-linking each other.

'You can mind-link with Reaper?' Magnus asks.

'One of my many abilities,' Alec adds sarcastically.

'What's he saying?'

'Reaper is advising I should join the pack,'

'And what did you say?'

'I told him I would do anything to get Nina back alive, even if that means becoming part of your stupid pack,'

'Well then, let's get you out of here and begin the initiation to join this stupid pack?'

Alec nods and watches Magnus take the keys and unlock the cell door. It creaks loudly as Magnus pulls it open and steps in. Alec and Magnus stand face to face on either side of the salt line. Magnus withdraws the athame from its sheath, 'Hold your hand out,' he says to Alec. Alec exposes the palm of his hand on his side of the line. Magnus extends his arm over the salt line to cut across the palm of Alec's hand, and then he cuts across his own palm. They firmly grip their hands together.

'I, Alpha Magnus, of the Shadow Crest Pack, with the Moon Goddess as our witness, accept Alec, the vampire king, into our pack. Wolf, Witch and now Vampire have merged.'

We hear the crack of lightning striking the coven stronghold and the severity of thunder and feel the gentle rumble of Pandora's Box beneath our feet. Then it all comes to an abrupt halt.

'The Moon Goddess approves.' Magnus announces aloud.

They part hands to find their wounds have all but healed.

Magnus sweeps the salt line away with his foot, and with a flash of speed, Alec is at the other side of the dungeon and awaits at the large inscribed door for freedom.

Chapter 33

Alec taps his feet anxiously as Magnus, Yiselda, and the other witches approach the final door that keeps Alec imprisoned.

'Are you certain you want to proceed, Alpha Magnus? There is no going back once I remove the sigils,'

'Do it,' Magnus commands unequivocally.

Yiselda brushes her palm across the door, obscuring the symbols, and trudges down the steps miserably. Magnus follows closely behind Alec as they walk through the mirror and continue out the front entrance of Pandora's box.

Alec falls to his knees, touches the ground, and raises his eyes to the sky. 'I never imagined the day would come when I would be delighted to see the day,' he says.

'Doesn't the sun harm you?' Magnus asks.

'No, but we aren't fond of it either. Vampires appreciate just one type of light: moonlight.

Otherwise,' Alec continues, 'We prefer to be out and about at night and inside during the day.'

Reaper pecks at the dirt near Alec's hands nonchalantly.

'Hmm, that's intriguing,' Magnus says.

'Let's waste no more time, take me to Shadow Crest so I can reclaim our Luna,' Alec says as he stands.

Magnus and Alec enter the circle, following the witches and appear at the packhouse.

'Alpha Magnus, I will not participate in your destruction of humanity. My immediate concern is for my sisters here, and I want to remain and defend them until Luna returns,' Yiselda informs him.

'I understand,' he replies.

All of the witches retreat to the basement.

May informs Magnus, 'I'm going with them,'

'All right, I'll mind-link you if I need you,' Magnus says.

'Sure,' she says, frowning as she walks away.

Alec takes a step toward Magnus.

'How do we get in contact with the wolf council?' Alec inquires.

'They reside in the north. It will take most of a day to get there,'

'Let us go to them. If we can eliminate the wolf council and save Nina, we can avoid harming the humans.' Magnus nods, shifts into his wolf, and dashes towards the woods, followed by Alec and Reaper.

After a night's travel, they arrive on the territory of the wolf council just as the sun rises. Wolves in the dozens approach us, growling and snapping to keep us at bay.

Alec stands unconcerned and smiles coyly, revealing his fangs. The wolves are taken aback and confused about what to do. Some turn and flee in fear. Most wolves remain put but are unsure if they should stay or run.

'I've come to retrieve my blood flame. Step aside or die!' Alec cautions.

Boisterous laughter comes from the wolf council's residence. The door swings wide to see Alpha Bennet chuckling. Alpha Theaton stands beside him. Alpha Amir reappears alongside Nina, holding a knife to her throat. A cloaked figure accompanies them.

'Alpha Magnus, I'm glad you kept your half of the agreement. Now Alec must do his share and kill the humans,' Alpha Bennet says.

Nina gasps, 'Alec, please don't do it,' she yells. Alpha Theaton smacks her hard against her face.

'Touch her again, and you will die!' Alpha Magnus yells.

Alec speeds ahead but comes to a halt when the hooded figure's enormous ball of flame spirals towards him.

Alec is unable to react quickly enough, and the flame strikes his arm, severely burning him. Alec hisses and tightens his grip on his arm. Alpha Amir puts the knife softly against Nina's neck, causing a trickle of blood to drip.

'Any closer and she dies,' Alpha Amir warns, 'I won't hesitate to cut her throat open. She wouldn't be the first she-wolf I've killed.' He smiles.

Alec takes a cautious step back, keeping his gaze fixed on Nina, who alternates her gaze wistfully between Alec and Magnus.

'Alec, he will kill Nina if we get any closer. Do you know who that hooded guy is and how he made that ball of fire?' Magnus asks.

'No idea. I'm just as stunned as you are,'

'Alpha Magnus,' Reaper corrects him through mind-link. Alec scoffs and rolls his eyes at Reaper.

'What is it?' Magnus asks.

'I think he might be a mage,' Reaper mind-links.

'Reaper says he could be a mage,'

'What? They exist too?' Magnus says.

'Yup.'

Alpha Bennet takes a step forward.

'I suggest you leave and not return until the humans are all dead,' Alpha Bennet yells. He steps towards Nina and hits her hard against her face causing her lip to bleed. 'The longer you delay, the more harm your precious Luna will sustain,'

Magnus and Alec exchange worried glances.

'If we approach Nina, Alpha Amir will kill her, and with the mage shielding them, we will be too late to stop Alpha Amir,' Magnus adds defeatedly.

'Then there is only one thing I can do to save her,' Alec says.

He holds his hands out and summons the Shadow Reapers and Grimghouls. They arrive in droves, ascending from the earth around us.

'If we approach a human city, they will deploy the army and all it possesses, including soldiers, tanks, and jets. What if I destroy their city without harming the civilians and lure the army to return here?

The wolf council and the mage would be caught in the crossfire, forced to battle for survival.

Perhaps this will provide us with an opportunity to rescue Nina while they fight? Additionally, they forget that when I attempted to exterminate humankind hundreds of years ago, they lacked the armament they possess now. Therefore, even if I desired to wipe out humanity with their bombs, chemical weapons, and arsenal, I would be unable to accomplish so,'

'You are right. None of this occurred to me. Why did you not bring this up earlier in the dungeon? You might have been released sooner if we had considered the strength of humankind now in comparison to centuries ago,'

Alec shrugs. 'I guess I was waiting for one of you to figure it out and realise I'm no longer as significant a threat as I once was. I hoped I would get the benefit of the doubt from someone, and I did, from Nina. She knew in her heart she could trust me.'

Magnus's expression transforms into one of remorse. 'She pleaded with me to release you, but I refused. I'm... sorry,'
'I'm sure you are,' Alec smirks. 'Now, let us proceed to make our presence known to humans.'

Magnus nods, shifts into his wolf and joins Alec, the Grimghouls and the Shadow Reapers in their pursuit of a large city.
Magnus mind-links May their plan.
'That might just work, Alpha. I'll put the television on and mind-link you to what the humans are planning. Yiselda has somewhat relaxed that she now knows you are only planning on destroying some buildings without harming humans. I'm worried, Alpha Magnus, even if we get Nina back safely. What will happen to us if the humans don't back down?'
'I'm not sure, May. We will worry about that part when we get to it.'

Chapter 34

Alec sends his minions to spread out on the first street they enter. The Grimghouls climb onto parked cars, rip the mirrors off and chew through the metal of the vehicles with ease as car alarms sound. Men, women and children run and scream. Then, the Shadow Reapers coalesce into a giant swirl of dark matter and flow beneath the vehicles, hurling them into the distance.

Alec makes sure there are no humans in the cars before they are tossed aside. Magnus shifts into his wolf and howls. All the humans watching are terrified and film what they can with their phones before fleeing.

Magnus chases after some of them, purposely running as slow as possible to allow them to escape. Police cars spread out along the street, and the officers shoot directly at the Grimghouls and Shadow Reapers while others radio for backup.

A helicopter soars high above them. It's from a News network.

'Magnus,' May mind-links, 'We can see you on the television. They are filming it all live and announcing the military is on its way. They are advising residents and shop owners to remain indoors and out of sight,'

'Perfect, as soon as the army arrives, we will draw them back to the territory of the wolf council,'

'Good luck, Magnus,' May mind-links.

More vehicles are flipped over, and street signs and poles are twisted. There is rubble from automobiles and buildings strewn everywhere.

After many hours, the military arrived, bringing tanks, aircraft, and soldiers.

'Stand down!' They shout.

Magnus howls at them, and something unexpected happens. They move so fast that I don't realise what they are until they approach Alec and me. Vampires.

They bow down to Alec, and the soldiers give each other a look as dozens more vampires approach and bow.

'Our king has been freed!' A female vampire announces.

'King?' The soldiers murmur to each other.

'I am Alec, vampire King!' Alec yells loudly with proudness.

'Master, give us your command,' a male vampire says.

Alec mind-links them to inform them that their queen, Nina, is in danger and that they must assist in luring the army to the territory of the wolf council without killing the humans. They nod and disperse across the street, just behind Alec and Magnus.

Alec and Magnus begin to retreat, giving the humans the illusion of victory. We are pursued and followed out of the city. Alec's strategy has thus far been successful. Alpha Bennet walks out of his house with a furious expression.

'Why did you bring the humans here!?' He yells.

Alec smiles, 'You want the humans wiped out? Carry it out yourself!' Alec shouts. The jets' bullets ricochet through the air, narrowly missing Alec and me.

Bullets have no effect on the Shadow Reapers since they go right through their silhouettes. Hundreds of pack members of the wolf council shift into their wolves and attack the soldiers.

Alec assists the soldiers by causing the werewolves' minds to be taken over by the Shadow Reapers. They instantly recognise one another as soldiers rather than werewolves. The werewolves cease attacking the soldiers and engage in fights with one another.

Alpha Bennet has ordered Kadva to help defend their premises.

Fireballs shoot through the air towards the jets, and the ground shakes violently at moments, causing humans to lose their footing. Soldiers are flung through the air as a result of his abilities. Alec directs the Grimghouls towards him, where he sees Alpha Bennet and Alpha Theaton fighting against the soldiers.

'Magnus, this is the time to find Nina while they are distracted.'

Magnus nods, and they hurry around the rear of the building, entering by the back entrance. They make their way toward a stairway.

'I can smell her scent. She must be down here,' Magnus says.

Alec sprints down the stairwell in a blink of an eye. Magnus hears Alpha Theaton's gargled final gasps. Alec has him pinned against the wall and drinks the blood from his neck. The cells are old and have a musty odour. Magnus scans the area and can see Nina unconscious in a nearby cell.

'Nina!' Magnus yells. He awkwardly grabs the key from Alpha Theaton's belt as Alec continues to drain the blood from his body. He runs to the cell door, unlocks it and kneels by Nina's side.

'Wake up, Nina. I'm here. You're safe now.' Magnus says, holding Nina in his lap. Then, in an instant, Alec appears next to them. As Nina stirs awake, Alec kneels and gently wipes her hair away from her face.

'Alec? Magnus?' She says, her eyes darting between them. She takes their hands in hers and cradles them to her bruised face. Taking in the overwhelming sense of sparks emanating from the bond she feels with each of them.

'We're here,' Alec smiles. Nina sits up and flings her arms around Magnus, kisses him endearingly, then turns to Alec and jumps up, wrapping her arms around his neck. They hold each other tight.

'Outside sounds like a warzone,' she murmurs.

'How did you get out of the dungeon? Oh! The humans! Please tell me you didn't?'

'No, Alec hasn't harmed the humans. Alec's idea was to make ourselves known in the city, destroy a few buildings and cars and lure the army to Alpha Bennet. They would have no choice but to fight against the humans, which would distract them from you. We used the opportunity to come down here and rescue you. I'm sorry, Nina, I should have listened to you earlier and let Alec out when you asked,' Magnus says.

'You let Alec out?' Nina says, surprised.

'Much to Yiselda's dismay,' Magnus laughs.

'Thank you,' she murmurs as she turns to Alec, who draws her into his chest and passionately kisses her.

'I have something for you,' Alec says and places her wand in her hand.

'How did you get this? Alpha Theaton took it from Kadva,' she says.

'Kadva?' Magnus and Alec say in unison.

'He is the mage you met earlier, unfortunately with a ball of fire. He is being forced to do Alpha Bennet's bidding. I'm sure of it,' Nina says with assertion. 'We need to put an end to the wolf council and Kadva and then convince the humans that we wish them no harm,'

'I'm not sure how well that will work, given that we did attack and destroy their city,' Alec says.

'We have to at least try.' Nina says as she makes her way to the stairwell. She gasps upon seeing Alpha Theaton's dead body with visible neck punctures.

'Don't look,' Alec says. Then taking Nina's hand, he leads her up the stairs.

They exit the building to see many dead wolves from the pack of the wolf council.

'I'll apprehend Kadva, and you two concentrate on defeating Alpha Bennet and Alpha Amir,' Nina says.

Magnus shifts into a wolf and sprints for Alpha Bennet, who is also in wolf form. Magnus lunges and knocks him to his side, biting his leg. Alpha Bennet leaps to his feet and savagely bites into Magnus's back, tearing a chunk of skin from his body. Magnus flips Alpha Bennet over and rips his stomach open with his claws.

May mind-links Magnus, 'Alpha, Pandora's Box, it's been destroyed. There is nothing left!'

'What do you mean it's gone?' He mind-links back.

'Yiselda returned there to grab a few items, and the entire coven stead was up in flames. She managed to port Star, her pets and the gnomes to Silverfay forest, but it was too late to save Pandora's Box. We soon discovered Hank nearby, attempting to flee. He was the one who started the fire. Yiselda was completely distraught. She killed Hank,'

'I'm sorry you all have lost your coven stead. Yiselda is part of our pack. Our home is always her home, too,' He mind-links back.

Alec fights Alpha Amir, appearing in front of him one moment and then the next moment behind Alpha Amir, throwing swift kicks and punches. Alec's movements are so fluid and quick that it nearly appears as though he is not moving at all. Alpha Amir collapses on the ground in defeat, just as a couple of Grimghouls tackle and rip him to pieces.

The soldiers are in utter disbelief and confusion as they watch the last of the werewolves killing each other, as well as Magnus, Alec and the vampires also killing the werewolves.

Nina sprints towards Kadva with her wand, 'Restraino Detainous,' A purple wind whirls around Kadva, lifting him off the ground and immobilising his arms and legs.

She approaches Kadva and removes his hood, takes a step back and gasps in surprise at Kadva's appearance.

Chapter 35

Kadva's eyes have an azure blue hue reminiscent of fine diamonds. His snow-white hair frames his heart-shaped face. He is a sight to behold, and he exudes exquisite beauty. He is young and appears to be around my age.

Reaper swoops down and settles on my shoulder.

'Kadva, it's all over now. The wolf council is no longer alive,' I tell him.

Kadva scans the strewn bodies and is taken aback to see the bodies of Alpha Bennet and Alpha Amir.

Kadva laughs, but in a relieved tone, 'They're dead?' He asks.

'Yes, but why were you following their orders?' I ask.

'They were going to inform the humans about me and the location of my whereabouts if I disobeyed their commands. I didn't want to be taken hostage and subjected to their experiments,'

'That's never going to happen, Kadva, now that they're gone. Do you have any friends or family?' I ask.

He shakes his head, 'No,' he says. 'I don't have anyone.'

Kadva places his hands on my head and says an incantation. I can now mind-link again.

I look to Magnus and Alec and Mind-link them, 'I think we should ask Kadva to join our pack? He is alone. He was afraid Alpha Bennet would hand him over to the humans for experimentation,' I explain.

Alec and Magnus exchange glances, then return their gaze to me and nod in agreement.

I wave my wand and break the spell on Kadva. He can now freely move his arms and legs. But, before I can ask him to join our pack, we are surrounded by soldiers.

'Stand down!' a soldier yells, 'Lower your weapons and put your hands on your head,'

Alec rushes forwards and appears in front of me in an instant. 'She is not coming with you,' Alec hisses. Grimghouls and Shadow Reapers reassemble behind me, prepared to strike the soldiers.

Magnus stands beside me in wolf form, growling at the troops. I rest my hand on his head and say, 'It's all right. I will speak with them and attempt to diffuse this situation, all right?' I say as I take a step forward in front of Alec.

'What are you doing, Nina?' He gently touches my arm.

'I want to speak with them,'

'Fine, but don't get any closer to them,' he says.

'My name is Nina, Luna of the Shadow Crest pack. I respectfully request that you lay down your firearms. We are not here to fight,' I exclaim.

The soldiers exchange glances and then return my gaze.

'Who or what are you? How did you get here?' A soldier shouts.

'I am half-werewolf and half-witch. Behind me stands Alec, the vampire king, and Magnus, the Alpha of Shadow Crest, and this is Kadva, the mage. We have been living here unnoticed and away from human society for centuries,'

The soldiers' exchange shocked mutterings.

'The wolf council is responsible for the attack on your city, but they have been eliminated. We hope to peacefully return to our territory and for you to return to yours,'

'Those two were in the city, causing chaos and destruction along with those creatures!' A soldier states pointing to the Grimghouls and Shadow Reapers.

'They didn't have a choice. They were forced into it,' I explain.

'Lies! They attacked us once. They will attack us again,' another shouts. They immediately begin firing at us. Alec envelops me in his cloak, lifts me, and vanishes into the distance. Magnus follows us in wolf form along with Kadva and Reaper. The Grimghouls and Shadow Reapers slow the soldiers down, allowing us time to escape.

I clutch Alec's shirt firmly and lay my head on his chest. He kisses my forehead.

'It feels incredible to have you back in my arms,' he smiles.

'It's good to be back in them and see you free of that dungeon,' I say.

I peer over his shoulder and notice Magnus is having difficulty keeping up. Something is wrong.

'Alec, please stop. Something is wrong with Magnus.'

He comes to a halt and gently places me down. I sprint over to Magnus and observe blood on his leg.

'Shift,' I tell Magnus.

When he shifts back, I see that a bullet has pierced his arm, and he is bleeding heavily.

'I'll be fine. We need to get back to Shadow Crest,' he says.

'No, the bullet is still in there. It will heal quickly if I remove it,'

Magnus sighs in defeat, and I dig two fingers inside the wound. Magnus masks the pain well. I remove the bullet. Over the next few minutes, the wound has sealed up and healed.

We shift into our wolves and run towards Shadow Crest with Alec, Reaper and Kadva following. It's the early hours of the morning when we arrive home. Kadva halts before entering the packhouse. He seems apprehensive.

'Kadva, you're with us now. We want you to join our pack,'

'You would welcome me into your pack?' His face brightens up with a smile. 'Even after I had kidnapped you?'

'You abducted me because you were forced to, but you never injured me, nor did you wish to hurt me,' I smile. 'Come on, let us have breakfast together.'

He gives me a nod and follows me into the packhouse. Yiselda, Fern, May, Lilac, Ela, and Ria dash down the stairwell. We all hug and weep at Pandora's Box's demise.

'I'm so sorry, Yiselda,' I frown.

'It's something I will have to learn to come to terms with, but I'm glad you are all safe and back home,' she says.

Yiselda raises an eyebrow at Alec and approaches him. 'Alec, I'm at a loss for words. I was certain you'd kill the humans, but you didn't. You proved me wrong, and I want to express my gratitude.' Alec nods but maintains silence.

'Who is this gorgeous gentleman!?' Lilac squeals, looking at Kadva, whose cheeks are now flushing from the witches' attention.

'Girls, this is Kadva. He is a mage and will be staying with us,' I explain.

They all squeal and crowd around him, flirtatiously stroking his arms, face, and chest.

'Um, help?' He says, his gaze fixed on me.

'Girls, cut him some slack. He has only arrived. I'm sure you'll all have plenty of opportunities to spend time with him, but for now, let's eat.' I say, taking my seat at the table.

We are all exhausted. We finish our breakfast. 'Kadva, Alec, we have more sleeping quarters upstairs. Follow me,' I say with a smile.

'This can be your room Kadva,' I say.

'Thank you. It's a nice room. I'm completely drained from travelling all night. 'I'm also going to sleep,' he says.

I show Alec the room next door to mine and Magnus's.

'You can sleep in this room,' Alec casts a perplexed glance. 'Is there a problem?' I ask.

'Vampires don't sleep,'

'Oh? Okay, so this may be the room that provides you with your own private space to have time alone?'

'This will be your room too?' He asks, hinting that he would desire to have me in there with him at times. I smile and nod.

Magnus tenderly takes my hand and leads me to our room. He carries me to our bed and covers me with kisses before we make intimate love and fall asleep.

Chapter 36

I awaken in the middle of the night and take a long shower. Magnus is sleeping soundly. I decide to venture outside to shift, allowing my wolf to run free. Reaper is asleep in the moon tree. As I ready myself to run, I feel warm sparks gliding down my spine. Alec is standing beside me, gently caressing the fur down my back as I turn my head.

'You are a lovely wolf,' he murmurs and kneels, and I rest my head on his lap while he pats me even more. 'May I join you on your run?' he inquires.

I nod and dash through the trees. Alec follows.

I can't believe I have my blood flame beside me. After all these years, he must feel relieved to be free of the dungeon. We sprint up the mountain and stop for a rest at the summit. I shift to my human state and lie in the grass. Alec approaches me, hovers over me, and locks his gaze with mine. Everything is perfect. My hand reaches out to brush across Alec's cheek. I draw his face closer to mine, and we kiss and make love passionately in the moonlight.

My head and hand are resting on his chest, and we are both staring at the moon. He caresses my arm, and we remain in this position for a short while.

Alec grins as he stands.

'What is it?' I ask.

'There is something I have always wanted to do with you,' he says.

'What is that?' I ask.

He takes my hand in his to assist me in standing. 'I want to dance with you under the stars right now.' He says.

His eyes glisten, and his gaze is filled with love and affection. I give a nod. He puts one hand around my waist and lifts the other, and we begin to waltz. I'm overcome with zeal and zest, and I can't help but smile shyly at Alec.

'I love you, Nina,' he smiles.

'I love you too, Alec,' I whisper.

Alec intensifies the waltz till we can't dance any longer. I giggle, and he laughs until we are both out of breath.

'The sun will shortly rise,' I smile, 'We should go back to the packhouse since I know you dislike the day,'

'As long as I'm with you, the day isn't that horrible.' He grins.

We travel down the hill holding hands. I come to a halt as I notice all the shadowy figures hidden amid the trees.

'Are they vampires?' I ask.

'Come and meet your Queen!' Alec shouts.

Several dozen Vampires emerge from the trees and bow in front of us. They then approach and kiss Alec's hand and then mine.

'Where did they come from, and where will they stay?' I ask.

'They have been hiding in many places away from people and supernatural beings, awaiting my return. They will stay close to me now that I am back, most likely here in these forests. Thus, enabling them to continue serving me in the manner they did hundreds of years ago,'

'Then I'd like to extend a warm welcome to Shadow Crest.' I say to them all. They nod, smile, and bow in unison.

As we make our way back to the packhouse, we hear the distant noises of helicopters and jets. Everyone exits the packhouse to investigate the sounds.

'They discovered us! But, how?' I panic.

Magnus mind-links the entire pack to get themselves ready to defend our territory. Our town is rocked by explosions. We turn to find a bomb has destroyed many houses. Other planes continue to fly above and release additional bombs. Soldiers in their hundreds approach, armed.

Kadva uses his abilities to keep them at bay with fireballs, while the witches and I use our spells against them, 'Repeliate!' I yell, sending a dozen troops into a brick wall. 'Tremendous Nebulous!' May casts, and the area suddenly becomes hazy, making it difficult for the soldiers to see us.

'Tumultuous Volley!' I say, a large cloud appears, and lightning strikes repetitively. Alec screeches, calling the vampires forth. They appear and help fight the soldiers, but hundreds more arrive. More bombs are dropped, destroying our whole village. Rubble and dust are strewn everywhere.

A tank is coming towards us, 'Inferno Flamo!' I yell. A massive ray of fire slams into the tank, completely engulfing it in flames. I feel my body beginning to weaken.

'Reaper,' I mind-link. 'Where are you? I need your power,'

'I'm trying to evade being struck by gunshots and explosives,' he mind-links. 'Incoming for landing,' he says as he crashes forcefully on my shoulder. His eyes blaze a brilliant white, and the black mist emanating from his body drifts into mine.

'Aqua Bedew!' I yell. A tornado of water arises and rips its way through the army of soldiers and collapses into a river of water, sweeping away numerous men into the nearby fields.

A dozen soldiers creep up behind Magnus as he battles against five other soldiers. 'Repeliate!' I shout, and they fly away into the air.

We are surrounded by destruction and death—a nearby soldier struggles for air. I kneel alongside him and grab hold of his vest, pulling him up.

'Tell me, how did you locate us?'

'Tell me now, or I will end your life for you,' I threaten the soldier.

He coughs out a small amount of blood.

'A few werewolves from the wolf council survived. They were weak and on the verge of death when they returned to human form. In exchange for sparing their lives, they revealed to us the exact location of each pack on a map. Army units have already been dispatched to all areas, and the majority have been annihilated,' he says.

I take a step back in horror, 'You're trying to kill us all?' I say with trepidation.

'Of course. You are all a threat to humankind with your magic abilities and capabilities of shifting.'

'You have to tell your men to stop, please,' I beg.

He laughs, 'Until you cease to exist, they will never stop.' He adds before collapsing. I take a step back and look at Alec, Magnus, and the others. Tears stream down my cheeks.

'He is right. The humans will never stop now that they know we exist,' I cry. They have destroyed Shadow Crest, and more military will arrive at any moment. We have two choices, stay and die or return to Mysteria?' I say.

'Mysteria?' Everybody says.

I make a beeline towards the packhouse. Due to an explosion, the left side has been destroyed. I enter my bedroom, retrieve my burlap sack, stuff it with a few spellbooks, and return outside with the book Mysteria: The history of supernaturals in my arms.

'I just finished reading this book a few days ago. It describes how supernatural beings originated from another dimension, a world known as Mysteria. When needed, a portal was opened, allowing humans to access Mysteria and supernatural beings to enter this world. When humans waged war in Mysteria, the portal was closed and has never been reopened since. They allowed the peaceful humans to stay but forced the remainder to return to earth. This book demonstrates how to open and close the portal,' I say, handing the book to Kadva.

He examines the page and then passes it to Yiselda.

'Do you believe we can open it?' I ask them.

Yiselda carefully reads the page. 'It takes a great deal of magic, Luna. But I think we can do it,'

Yiselda sets the open book flat on the ground and extends her hands.

'Let's do this,' Yiselda says.

'There is something I need to do first,' Alec says. He opens the portal to Silverfay forest and summons the Grimghouls and the Shadow Reapers. One by one, the Grimghouls jump through the portal and change back into their pixie forms. Once they have returned to Silverfay forest, he closes the portal, faces the Shadow Reapers, and raises his hands. Black swirls emit from his hands, and another portal opens, revealing a vast graveyard. The Shadow Reapers enter the portal and return to their resting places.

'After all this time, all I had to do to change them back into their natural forms was return them to Silverfay forest and the graveyard they came from?' Yiselda growls.

Alec smirks and nods at her.

Chapter 37

I take Yiselda's hand, and Kadva takes my other hand. Then, fern, May, Lilac, Ela and Ria join the circle. Once we are connected, holding hands, Yiselda begins the chant. We repeat the words repeatedly until our eyes start to glow one by one. I can feel my energy, my magic being drained from my body. I'm feeling overwhelmingly weak. The others are also struggling to hold their footing. Finally, Reaper gives me his power, helping me to regain strength. The portal begins to open.

'I see it, keep going, Magnus,' yells. The witches fall to their knees but keep a firm hold of each other's hands. As the portal opens further, I see many people staring curiously at us. Some have different brightly coloured eyes, and then I noticed some are bulky with green skin and tusks.

A beautiful young woman with long black hair and violet eyes approaches along with a large handsome man with brown hair. Another in armour approaches with scruffy black hair and a few scars on his face. Horses gallop by with the green-skinned riders carrying jousts. One has a broken tusk. There are purple and gold flags, and everyone is dressed in medieval attire. Then I realised the portal had opened in the midst of a jousting competition in Mysteria.

'Magnus, get any surviving pack members to jump through the portal now and Alec, same with the vampires.'

Several dozen pack members, including my parents, Ryker, Astrid, Flint, and Josie, leap through. When we let go of each other's hands, the doorway will begin to close.

I yell to the others, 'We will be the last to leap over,'

'Alec, Magnus, you must go. We will follow both of you,'

'No,' they both say together. 'We aren't going through unless it's with you,' Magnus says. Alec nods at him in agreement.

I let go of Yiselda and Kadva's hands. 'Quick! Go, it's already beginning to close!' I yell. Yiselda and Kadva jump through, then Lilac, May, and Ria with their familiars. Then Ela and Fern with their familiars.

Alec grabs my hand, and Magnus takes the other, and we leap through the portal together, landing on the grass in front of the beautiful young lady with violet eyes.

The gateway has been closed, and we take in our surroundings with wonder.

'Is this Mysteria?' I ask, gazing up at the stunning young lady.

'Yes,' she giggles sweetly.

'I notice you've brought several companions?' She gives a kind smile.

'Be careful, Luna, they might be dangerous,' the older man with untidy black hair in armour warns.

'I can sense their wolves, Sir Hugo, which implies they are one of us. However, this one a wolf and something else?' She says, lowering her gaze to mine.

'You're a Luna too?' I ask. She nods.

'I am Maia, Luna and Queen of Mooncrest, and this is my mate Damon, the King and Alpha of Mooncrest,'

I stand up with Alec and Magnus, and we shake their hands.

'We are so happy to meet you, this is Magnus, my mate and Alpha of Shadow Crest, and this is Alec, my blood flame, King of vampires. My name is Nina, Luna of Shadow Crest and Queen of the vampires,' I say.

Maia squeals, 'Did you hear that, darling? Another Luna that's also a queen,' she says to Alpha Damon. He nods and smiles at us.

Reaper caws in annoyance.

'Oh, and this is my familiar, Reaper,'

'Charmed,' she says to Reaper with a bow.

'You came through a portal that hasn't been open for over a thousand years. What has brought you back here to Mysteria? We could see a lot of destruction through the portal,' Alpha Damon says.

'Humankind found out about supernaturals. They refused to stop killing us until we were all dead because they feared our power. So they destroyed all the packs. Our only option to live was to try and open the portal and return here,' I say.

'You did the right thing by returning to Mysteria, where your origins began. Alpha Damon and I will see that you all have a place here to call home.

A red-headed, freckled lady jumps up behind Maia, 'What's going on?' she asks.

'Oh, Ember, you're in for a treat!' Maia says.

'Oh?' she exclaims. Confusion sets in as she takes in all the unfamiliar faces.

'This is Nina, Luna of Shadow Crest, Queen of Vampires, half-wolf and half-witch!' Maia exclaims.

Ember's expression is a mixture of disbelief and joy as she sprints toward me and wraps her arms around my neck.

'Another witch, and she's my age as well!' Ember joyfully screams.

'It's a pleasure to meet you, Ember. I am not the only witch here,' I smile. 'Acquaint yourself with May, Fern, Lilac, Ela, Ria, and Yiselda!' I say.

Ember screams in joy and passes out.

Maia laughs, 'Don't mind, Ember, she is the oldest witch here. All the other witches are children,' she explains.

A cute green skinned little boy with tiny tusks approaches us.

‘Hello there,’ I smile, ‘What’s your name?’

'My name is Drudge, and when I grow up, I want to be a warrior,' he adds, fist-pumping his chest.

'Nice to meet you, Drudge. My name is Nina, and judging by the muscles you currently possess, you will be an excellent warrior,' I grin.

Drudge triumphantly straightens himself and walks away.

'Drudge is an Orc,' Alpha Damon states,

‘Orcs! How fantastic,' I exclaim.

I assist in reawakening Ember, and she sprints up to the witches, shouting, 'Group hug!' They chuckle, and joke at her antics yet appreciate her embrace.

'How did you meet Alpha King Damon, and why are all the witches here, children?' I ask.

'It's a long story,' Maia shrugs. 'The tale of the Alpha King and me,' she smiles.

'I'd be delighted to hear it,' I say.

'Then I shall begin the story,' Maia smiles

To Be Continued.

Book Four: The Alpha King’s Mate

ABOUT THE AUTHOR

Jazz Ford is a wife and mother of three children. She lives in Geelong, Victoria, Australia. She is a former Personal Care Attendant, with a background in nursing homes and in-home care. She loves writing full-time from home. In her spare time, she enjoys photography, graphic design and spending time with her husband and children. Jazz Ford's other works are 'The Alpha's Mate Who Cried Wolf', 'The Alpha Who Cursed His Mate', 'Alpha Maximus: The Last Lycan' 'Love, Vogue and the CEO,' and many more. You can find Jazz on TikTok, and Facebook.

Printed in Great Britain
by Amazon

17138570R00169